Four Silences Broken

Four Silences Broken

A Secrets of Hartwell Novel

H L Marsay

TULE
PUBLISHING

Acknowledgements

My thanks as always to the wonderful team at Tule: Jane Porter, Meghan Farrell, Cyndi Parent and Nikki Babri.

I was very lucky to work with three amazing editors again: Sinclair Sawhney, Helena Newton and Marlene Roberts. Many thanks for all your suggestions and your support.

A big thank you also to Lee Hyat for coordinating the beautiful book cover design.

The human heart has hidden treasures,
In secret kept, in silence sealed;
The thoughts, the hopes, the dreams, the pleasures,
Whose charms were broken if revealed.

Charlotte Brontë 1816–1855
Yorkshire

CHAPTER ONE

A SHARP BLAST of wind sent the brown and gold leaves swirling across the cobbles. Lucy Hanley pulled her coat a little tighter around her as she hurried into the village shop. Thanks to Nora, the miserable shopkeeper, she normally tried to avoid the place, but it was Bonfire Night and she'd forgotten to buy some sparklers on her weekly trip to the supermarket in Thirsk. Freddie had said he didn't mind, but she still felt guilty. They never let off fireworks. When Rupert was alive, he'd complained that they were a waste of money and now Freddie was older, he worried they would scare the dogs. In fact, he and his best friend, Krish, were campaigning to make Hartwell a firework-free zone.

Not that they wouldn't still be celebrating. Rob had helped the boys build a bonfire in the field behind the village hall. They had invited the rest of the village to attend providing they promised not to let off fireworks and Jack, from the White Hart, was providing hot dogs and burgers. All Lucy had to do was buy the sparklers and she'd managed to mess that up.

The shop bell jangled loudly as she stepped inside. Fortunately, the place was quite busy with other Hartwell residents. She nodded 'hello' to a few people she knew as she made her way to the back of the shop. Quickly, she rummaged through the fairly paltry selection of overpriced Roman candles and Catherine wheels on a shelf until she found some packets of sparklers.

"Well! I didn't think we'd be seeing you today. I thought you'd be keeping a low profile!" said an all too familiar voice behind her. Lucy cringed, then took a deep breath, switched on a bright smile and turned to face Nora.

"Why is that, Mrs Parkin?" she asked politely. Nora's sour face looked almost triumphant as she held up two of the morning newspapers. On the front page of the tabloid was a photo of Sadie, Lucy's mother, looking beautiful but striking a tragic pose, beneath the headline 'Sadie's Heartbreak Over Daughter's Rejection'.

"Talk about washing your dirty laundry in public," crowed Nora. "And thanks to you it looks like we are going to have to choose a new MP. Heaven only knows if they'll be any good or not!"

Lucy's gaze travelled to the front of the broadsheet, and she almost shuddered when she saw the face of Guy Lovell grinned back at her. His photo was accompanied by the more subdued title 'Date Set For Local By-Election'. Lucy's eyes flicked between the two pictures. She felt her mouth go dry and her cheeks begin to burn. She hadn't heard from her mother since she'd kicked her out after she'd attempted, unsuccessfully, to seduce Rob when he was in bed with concussion. As for Guy, the last time she'd seen him, he'd been threatening her with a gun.

The other customers were starting to stare, and Nora was clearly expecting a response, but Lucy didn't say a word.

Instead, she pushed past the shopkeeper, slapped the money for the sparklers down on the counter and hurried out the door. She almost ran back to Dizzy, her ancient four-wheel drive, and dumped the sparklers on the passenger seat, but before she could drive off, there was a tapping on her window. It was Colonel Marsden, smiling beneath his trilby and brandishing the two newspapers. A little reluctantly, Lucy opened her door.

"I don't blame you for not wanting to respond to Mrs Parkin, my dear. Catching you in an ambush like that, but I thought you might still want to read these," he said thrusting the papers towards her.

"Thank you," said Lucy with a grateful smile. "I probably should find out what's going on."

"Absolutely! Forewarned is forearmed and all that. Good day!" The elderly ex-soldier politely raised his hat then limped away, his three dogs trotting obediently behind him.

Lucy laid the newspapers next to the sparklers. Her mother's face stared back at her. She read the first few lines of the article. Apparently, Sadie had written her autobiography and the newspaper was planning on serialising it over the coming weeks. The first instalment was going to be about 'her troubled relationship with her estranged, aristocratic daughter'. Despite herself, Lucy had worried about how Sadie, who was broke after a life of decadence, would be able to pay her way. Now she knew.

With a heavy sigh she turned on the ignition and drove back along the puddle-strewn road to Hartwell Hall. The elegant and imposing stone building that stood on the edge of the village had been her home since she married Rupert, and she loved the old place even if maintaining it was a full-time job. Now, after a lot of hard work, she was finally finding a way to make the Hall to pay for itself. She had been hiring the house and grounds out for weddings and other events. A film company had even used it as location for a new adaptation of *Jane Eyre*. Then just as life seemed to be running smoothly, Sadie and Guy came back to disrupt everything. As she passed the gatehouse she could see Joan, her housekeeper, bringing in the washing that had been drying on the line. She stopped and wound down her window.

"Oh dear. What's happened?" asked Joan as soon as she saw the troubled look on Lucy's face.

"Sadie strikes again," replied Lucy holding up the tabloid newspaper.

Joan frowned and shook her head. "That woman! Now don't you go getting upset, love. You know what they say. Today's front pages are tomorrow's fish and chip paper."

Lucy drove on feeling a little better. Joan and her husband, Bill, who looked after the gardens at the Hall, had been more like family to her than Sadie ever had. But she supposed she could thank her mother for one thing—her getting together with Rob. Sadie pouncing on him when he was asleep had finally made the two of them admit how they felt about each other. Since then, they had barely been apart and Lucy had been happier than she'd been in years.

Dizzy trundled down the long driveway, bumping over the potholes that seemed to have appeared after the first frost of the year. Her arrival in the vast kitchen, in what had once been the servants' quarters, was met with loud barking from

Tilly and Pickle. Rob was sitting at the kitchen table looking at a set of plans for his latest development.

"Did you get the sparklers? Uh-oh, what's wrong?" he asked when he looked up. She'd never been any good at hiding her feelings.

"Where's Freddie?" she whispered still clutching the papers to her chest. She didn't want her son to see either article.

"Giving Root a bath. He rolled in something on his walk and was stinking the place out. Why? What's up?" Rob's handsome face creased in concern. Lucy placed the newspapers on the table and pushed them towards him. Rob's dark blue eyes scanned both the front pages. Then he raised an eyebrow and wordlessly picked them up and dropped them in the bin.

"I haven't read them yet," Lucy protested.

"You don't need to. I can guarantee there is nothing in those pages that will improve your day."

"The colonel said forewarned is forearmed," said Lucy chewing her lip as she often did when she was anxious.

"Forearmed for what?" asked Rob.

"I'm not sure. So, I know what Mum is going to put in her book, I suppose."

"It'll be a load of rubbish," he said as he wrapped his arms around her and placed a kiss on top of her head. "At least you know she isn't, how did you put it, 'starving in a gutter somewhere'."

Lucy smiled despite herself. Rob, who preferred to use as few words as possible, always teased her for being overly dramatic.

"What about the article about Guy?"

"It won't tell you anything you don't know," he said gently. "He hasn't left the psychiatric hospital since he was arrested. It was obvious he had to stand down as an MP. In a few weeks, the court case will be over, and we can put the whole thing behind us."

"There might have been some news about the by-election. Aren't you at least interested in who is going to be standing?"

"Nope. It doesn't matter who we end up with. Politicians are all the same. They promise you the world at election time and deliver nowt. Nothing will change."

"I didn't know you were so cynical."

"I'm not. I'm just saying how it is."

At that moment, Freddie appeared with a dripping wet Root wrapped in a towel in his arms.

"Oh dear, he looks rather sorry for himself," said Lucy. Freddie put his puppy down next to the Aga and Root promptly shook and showered them all in water.

"I think he preferred smelling of fox poo," said Freddie.

"Well, thank goodness he doesn't anymore. The girls are coming over for lunch," replied Lucy as she suddenly remembered she needed to defrost the lasagne Joan had made earlier in the week. Over the summer, she had been so busy with the estate and Sadie and trying to keep a low profile, she felt she'd neglected her friends. She was determined to make amends. Rob and Freddie exchanged an amused look as Lucy cautiously removed the plastic lid covering the dish.

"What do you think, Freddie? Is that our cue to go and

get lunch at the pub?" asked Rob.

"Yay!" replied Freddie enthusiastically. "Then can we check on the bonfire?"

"Again?" enquired Lucy looking up for a second.

"Yes," replied Freddie looking very serious. "We need to check there aren't any hedgehogs hibernating in it. And don't forget we are lighting it at five, so don't be late."

"We'll see you later," said Rob with a grin as he planted a goodbye kiss in the crook of her neck. "Have fun with the girls. Give them our love."

"Can we see if Ben and Krish want to come too?" asked Freddie, already reaching for his coat. "See you later, Mum."

The two of them disappeared out the door, leaving Lucy with a damp dog and only half an hour to prepare. She smiled to herself as she bunged the dish in the oven and grabbed the towel to mop up the trail of water Freddie and Root had no doubt left through the house. In the few months since she and Rob had got together, he had been more of a father to her son than Rupert had been when he was alive. She often worried about how his parents' troubled relationship, and then Rupert's death, might have affected Freddie, but he certainly seemed happy enough.

RACHEL WAS THE first to arrive.

"Hi, Luce, are you okay?" her friend greeted her with a hug. "I read about your mum and Guy in the papers this morning. Did you see?"

Lucy rolled her eyes. "Nora took great delight in telling

me all about it."

"Ugh, that woman gets worse," replied Rachel with a grimace. "The other day we were having a quiet drink in the Hart, and she had the cheek to ask me if my cottage wasn't too poky to accommodate a lodger."

"What did you say?"

"I told her it didn't bother us as we spent most of our time in my king-size bed."

Lucy's hand flew to her mouth. "You didn't?"

"I did. The old bag nearly choked on her sherry."

"I wish I'd been there." Lucy laughed. "Is Sarah not with you?"

"No, I tried to get her to come, but she's working. I swear, one of these days she's going to need to be surgically removed from that laptop."

Sarah had moved in with Rachel at about the same time Lucy had got together with Rob. She was an archaeologist at York University and arrived in the village when Rob's team of builders had unearthed an ancient Druid burial site.

Jo and Meera arrived at the same time. Both had been at work that morning. Meera, the village doctor, was dressed in a smart shift dress and jacket. In contrast, Jo, who had been reluctantly relocated to North Yorkshire from Scotland Yard, was wearing jeans, a polo neck and a slightly battered biker jacket. Meera was carrying two large Tupperware containers.

"I hope you don't mind," she said, "but I brought some samosas and pakoras. You know I always get carried away and make too much when I start cooking."

"Meera, you are an angel!" said Lucy, gratefully taking the two containers as she kissed her friend on the cheek. "I must admit, I might have left it a little late to put the lasagne in the oven. There's a good chance it might be cold in the middle so these will be perfect."

Jo handed over a bag from the off-licence in Thirsk.

"I brought some of that fizzy crap you drink. The beer is for me."

Lucy went in search of some glasses and plates while the others chatted in the library, the only room in Hartwell Hall that could be called cosy. She'd missed this. As much as she loved spending time with Freddie and Rob, it was good to have her friends here again. Jo with her no-nonsense approach to life, Rachel's humour and Meera, who was often a lifesaver in more ways than one.

When she returned to the library, they were all settled around the roaring fire chatting. There was plenty to catch up on: Rachel's half-term holiday to Greece, Jo's recent birthday trip back to London with Jack, and Meera's forthcoming wedding to Ben. It was going to have a Regency theme and the other three were to be her bridesmaids. Lucy was thrilled by the idea of dressing up like a character from Jane Austen; Jo and Rachel, less so. After Jo had demolished the last samosa, Lucy cleared the plates away and went to fetch a second bottle of prosecco.

"Lucy, we were just saying how lovely the place is looking," said Meera, as Lucy handed her another mineral water.

"It's all thanks to the film company. They were so pleased with the way *Jane Eyre* turned out, they want to use the place again for *Emma*."

Meera clapped her hands together in delight, she was a huge fan of both the Brontës and Austen. Lucy grinned.

"I knew you'd be excited. The money from their contract meant I could finally afford to replace the most rotten windows in here and next week the roofers Rob found for me are starting work on retiling. It will be such a relief not to have to dash around with buckets every time there is a downpour. That reminds me, I was clearing some of the bedrooms in the west wing before the builders start and I found loads of photos in the back of one of the wardrobes." She retrieved an old shoebox from behind the sofa and tipped the contents on to the table. "Look at this one of your mum, Rachel. I swear she barely looks a day older."

They all leaned forward and peered at a crinkled-edged photo of four women sitting together in the library in exactly the same spot as they were now, smiling up at them.

"They look like us," commented Jo.

"You're right—Mum does look the same," said Rachel. "And Joan has hardly changed either."

"Who's that?" asked Meera.

"Shirley when she used to dye her hair blonde and wear it in a beehive," said Rachel. "I remember her putting on a cabaret in the Hart every Friday, back when Jack's dad was alive. She's always loved performing."

"Is that Caroline? She's smiling—I barely recognised her," said Jo, pointing to the fourth woman in the picture. Lady Caroline Hanley was Lucy's formidable mother-in-law, who although she now lived at the dower house, still acted like she was in charge of Hartwell Hall and its estate. "They look pretty close. I didn't know they were all such good friends," replied Jo.

Rachel picked up the photo and squinted at it. "Is Caroline pregnant or is it the dress she's wearing? I've only ever known her to be as thin as a whippet."

"Maybe it's when she was expecting Rupert," suggested Meera. "Who's that crawling around on the rug?"

"It's Jack, I think," said Rachel, studying the chubby, dark-haired toddler, who was now the landlord of The White Hart and Jo's boyfriend.

"Caroline can't be pregnant then," said Lucy. "Jack and Rupert were born within a few weeks of each other. Is there a date on the back?"

Rachel turned it over.

"It was taken in June thirty years ago," she read.

"So, Rupert, Jack and I would all have been toddlers," said Rachel. "I wonder where I am and who took the photo."

"Perhaps it was Rupert's father?" suggested Meera. "He was called Alexander, wasn't he?"

"Yes, but I doubt he was here then," replied Lucy. "At the time he was working for the foreign office. Caroline said he spent most of his time in London or at some embassy or other when Rupert was little. Besides, although he died before I had the chance to meet him, he didn't sound like the type of man who would sit around with his wife's friends taking jolly snaps."

"Is Mary pregnant with Becky?" asked Meera.

Rachel frowned. "No, she wasn't born until two years later. Mum must be going through one of her plump phases. She was always prone to putting on weight like me. You've only known her when she's been at her thinnest. She dropped two stone after losing Dad. It must have been the shock."

Meera nodded sympathetically and Jo yawned loudly.

"Are we boring you?" asked Rachel arching an eyebrow sarcastically.

"Sorry," said Jo, yawning again. "I was working nights last week, and I've been knackered ever since. Last night I fell asleep at eight o'clock."

"You do look a little pale. You should take better care of yourself," chided Meera.

"I'm fine, but I need to catch up on some sleep. I'll go home for a snooze before the bonfire," she said standing up. "Thanks for feeding me, Luce. I'll see you all later."

Lucy walked Jo to her car while Rachel and Meera stayed by the crackling fire looking at the old photos.

A couple of hours later, as it was growing dark, they pulled on their hats and coats and set off for the village hall. Meera, who had only been drinking mineral water, drove them down there.

"Is Sarah going to meet us there?" Lucy asked Rachel.

"I hope so. I'm sending her a text," replied Rachel from the back seat as she tapped at her phone.

When they arrive at the village hall, it looked like most of Hartwell had turned out. Certainly, all Krish and Freddie's classmates and their parents had come to support the boys. Lucy waved to Jack who was inside the hall, preparing the food. Jo, who still looked a little pale after her nap, was helping him.

Before they lit the bonfire, Krish and Freddie gave a little speech thanking everyone for coming and explaining why they wanted to make the night firework free. Lucy thought she might burst with pride as she watched her little boy looking and sounding so grown-up. She felt a hand on her arm and turned to see Meera dabbing at her eyes.

"Wasn't that wonderful?" she whispered. "I do hope Ben has videoed it."

Then the crowd burst into applause as Rob helped the two boys light the huge bonfire. As the flames crackled and leapt into the dark November night, Lucy handed out the sparklers and laughed as she watched the boys try and write their names in gold and silver. Rob came and wrapped his arm around her.

"Happy?" he asked.

"Very," she whispered back. "At the risk of sounding like Freddie, I think this might be the best Bonfire Night ever."

Several hours and far too many hot dogs later, the three of them returned to Hartwell Hall and were greeted noisily by the dogs.

"It's a good thing it's not a school night," said Lucy, attempting to sound stern.

"But I think everyone had a good time and I didn't see one firework going off, so our plan worked," said Freddie, yawning widely.

"Well done. Now straight up to bed," said Lucy with a smile.

"Does that apply to me too?" Rob whispered in her ear as Freddie disappeared up the stairs.

The longcase clock at the foot of the stairs struck midnight, but Lucy was still awake. She reached out and picked up her phone from the bedside table. Despite telling herself it was a bad idea, she couldn't resist taking a look at the tabloid newspaper's website and read the first instalment of her mother's autobiography. She began scrolling through, but it was more about her than Sadie. Although her mother had been a notorious party girl with a string of famous boyfriends, she had chosen to launch her book by spilling all her daughter's secrets instead.

It was all there. How Lucy's fairy-tale wedding had turned into a nightmare thanks to Rupert's drug addiction. Then how he had disappeared during lockdown and his body was eventually found months later in a cave. The financial struggle Lucy had faced to keep the estate solvent. How she had turned to her friend Guy, for advice and support, only to discover he was a deranged stalker. There were intimate details that Lucy had told her mother in confidence, but that obviously wasn't important to Sadie. She even dragged Rob in at the end, referring to him as a 'handsome rogue' with 'a violent past', who had come between her and her beloved daughter.

It was a total lie. Rob had gone to prison for protecting his sister and the only person who had ruined their mother-daughter relationship was Sadie herself. Lucy felt sick. She quickly put the phone down and snuggled closer to Rob, who was gently snoring. He had been right. It was better to leave her mother and all she had to say in the past. She wouldn't let her spoil a wonderful evening.

CHAPTER TWO

"WHICH DO YOU prefer for the drawing room, Solway Storm or Southwold Pebble?" asked Meera as she and Ben finished breakfast a few days later. She held up the paint colour chart.

Ben adjusted his glasses, bent down and squinted. "I'm sorry, Meera. I can't see any difference. They both look grey to me."

Meera pursed her lips. "Really? You don't think the first is more blue?"

Ben's phone bleeped. He checked the screen. "Sorry, I have to go up to Dan's farm. His daughter's pony has colic." He quickly dropped a kiss on top of her head. "You choose whichever one you think is best. I'm sure it will be perfect."

He grabbed his coat and bag and hurried out of the door. Meera watched him go then made her way out of the kitchen and across the hall to the drawing room, frowning slightly. She loved Ben very much. He had many wonderful qualities. He was an amazing vet, and he would be an even more amazing stepfather to Krish, but sometimes she thought he would be quite happy to paint every room in the Grange magnolia.

"Mr Linter? In here, please could we have Solway Storm

below the dado rail and Southwold Pebble above? The rail itself to picked out in Antiguan Sand," she said decisively as she entered the dust-sheet-strewn drawing room.

"Whatever you like, Mrs Bannister."

This was the slightly doddery decorator's response to almost everything Meera said. He always referred to her this way. Countless times she'd tried to explain that she and Ben weren't married yet, her professional name was Dr Kumar, but she was happy for him to call her Meera. It did no good. Eventually, Meera had given up. She also tried not to get stressed about the fact that Mr Linter never wrote any of her instructions down. He had been recommended by Rob, who had used him to decorate the Hayloft, the property he had converted down by the village hall.

The original plan had been for Ben, with the assistance of Krish, to tackle the decorating themselves. Meera had approved of the idea of saving money and liked the thought of the two men in her life bonding as they transformed their new home. The first room they had tackled was Krish's bedroom. It was a disaster. Ben's glasses had managed to fall into a tin of paint. Then they'd left a tray of emulsion on the floor that Darwin, the ferret, ran through leaving a trail of tiny blue paw prints over the newly sanded and polished floorboards. In despair, Meera had told them they would have to call in a professional and so far she hadn't regretted it.

Two months after moving in, there were only a few rooms left to decorate and with luck they should be finished before their wedding that was due to take place a week before Christmas.

AFTER SETTING MR Linter to work, Meera dropped Krish off at school before beginning the series of house calls she was scheduled to make that morning. He gave her a cheerful wave as he dashed across the playground to meet Freddie. Since arriving in Hartwell, her quiet, shy little boy had become so confident and she'd seen a vast improvement in the asthma that had plagued his childhood. She had been so proud watching him make his speech in front of all those people and that he had worked so hard campaigning for something that he thought was important. He had always adored animals and, together with Freddie, he had convinced the rest of the village not to set off fireworks because they caused distress to both pets and wildlife. Almost everyone in Hartwell had supported the idea; in fact, several local farmers had approached her and asked her to pass on their thanks to Krish.

"It's the first fifth of November I haven't had to call Ben out," Dan Foxton, Rachel's cousin had said. "At least one of my herd usually gets spooked and injures themselves running away."

First on her list was Colonel Marsden. He had phoned the surgery yesterday to say that his gout had flared up and he was unable to walk to his appointment. Following his precise instructions, Meera let herself into Beck House, the colonel's Georgian house that could only be accessed via a bridge over the village stream. Her arrival was greeting by loud barking from his three dogs, but they were silenced by a sharp command from their master. She found him in the snug, wearing a tartan dressing down and sitting in an armchair with his foot resting on a padded stool.

"Good morning, Colonel," said Meera politely. "How is your foot?"

"Take a look for yourself, Doctor," he replied, looking rather sorry for himself. Meera gently lifted the bag of frozen peas he had placed on the offending toe. She winced. The skin around the big toe was horribly red, hot and very swollen.

"I'm going to prescribe you some steroids," she said. "I want you to keep resting and drinking plenty of water. The swelling should go down in a day or two."

"That's all very well, Doctor, but what about the dogs? They need regular exercise or they get restless, like the troops. If you don't keep them occupied that's when they get up to mischief."

Meera glanced over to the three black Labradors, who were lying in a neat row next to the colonel watching her intently.

"I understand," she said. "I'll ask around and see if someone can help. Now, I think I should take your blood pressure while I'm here."

"Well, if you must, but it's bound to be high with all this stress," he grumbled, rolling up his sleeve. He was right.

"One hundred and forty over ninety," reported Meera sternly.

"Now don't start telling me to cut down on alcohol and salt again, Doctor. We've all got to die sometime, and a man has to have some pleasures in life," grumbled the colonel.

Meera let herself out. She didn't blame him for being so

grumpy. The poor man was alone and in a lot of pain. Her next call was Reverend Davenport, who was also incapacitated. He had sprained his ankle after slipping on the church steps following the first frost of the year. The door of the vicarage was opened by a large, jolly-looking woman. With her mop of short white hair and large round glasses, she reminded Meera of the barn owls Krish was so fond of spotting.

"Hello, can I help you?" she asked brightly. Her voice had a slight Durham accent.

"Hello, I'm Dr Kumar. I'm here to see Reverend Davenport."

"Are you? That's nice. He does like company." She pumped Meera's hand up and down several times. "I'm Belinda, by the way. I'm the new curate. I'll be taking the services until he's back on his feet again."

Meera followed Belinda through the vicarage. From the outside, it was a pretty, well-proportioned house, built in mellow York stone; but inside it was like a 1970s time warp, with woodchip on the walls and an ugly carpet with brown swirls. Reverend Davenport was in the sitting room, lying on an orange velour sofa, tucked under a duvet with a tray of tea and chocolate biscuits next to him. He was chuckling to himself as he watched an old Ealing comedy on the ancient television in the corner. He looked up in surprise when he saw Meera.

"Hello there, Doctor. This is a nice surprise. Forgive me for not getting up to greet you—I've injured my foot, you know."

Meera felt a little perplexed at his greeting. He'd phoned

the surgery yesterday in quite an agitated state, insisting he needed to see someone.

"Yes, I do know about your foot, Reverend. You telephoned to say you thought it was getting worse," she said, gently.

The old man frowned. "Did I, my dear? How very odd. I was only saying this morning that it feels much better today, wasn't I, Belinda?"

The curate nodded and smiled encouragingly. "Yes, you did, Michael."

"Would you mind if I took a quick look anyway?" asked Meera.

"Not at all. Be my guest, Doctor."

Meera carefully lifted the duvet to expose his ankles. The bruising and swelling had almost totally disappeared.

"It looks a lot better," she confirmed, "and if you aren't in any pain, I'll be on my way."

"Won't you stay for a cup of tea?" offered Belinda.

Meera shook her head. "No thank you, I still have another visit to make." She turned back to the reverend. "You should be back on your feet very soon, but take things easy at first."

"I certainly will, Doctor. It was very nice to see you. God bless," he replied cheerfully.

Belinda lowered her voice as she walked Meera to the door. "I am very sorry, Doctor. He does get a little confused and forgetful these days. His mobile is on the table next to him, so I don't always know if he's made a call. The other day he called the village store complaining they hadn't delivered the newspaper, but it was laid right next to him. I think that's partly why the diocese sent me here, to help look after him."

Meera frowned. "That sounds a little worrying. Perhaps he should come in for some tests when his ankle has healed."

"I think that would be an excellent idea, Doctor."

"Does he have any family?" asked Meera.

"There is a niece, who lives in France. I contacted her after his fall. She's away on business at the moment, but she's promised to come and see him as soon as she can."

"Good," replied Meera. "And in the meantime, do let me know if you have any concerns."

Belinda waved her goodbye and Meera left the vicarage wondering if the reverend's confusion was simply due to shock following his fall—he had bumped his head—or something more sinister. She couldn't help thinking that although Reverend Davenport's surroundings might not be as grand as the colonel's, she would rather be in his position with the kind and jolly Belinda there to take care of him, than alone except for his dogs.

A loud rumbling sound caught her attention. On the other side of the street, several large barrels of beer were being rolled over the cobbles to the White Hart. Jack, the landlord was taking delivery. He was a large, bear-like man, who had once been a professional rugby player, until a knee injury had ended his career.

He greeted Meera with a huge grin. "I'm sorry, Meera. I know you like to start the day with a double whisky, but we don't open until eleven."

"Very funny," laughed Meera, who was used to his teasing, "but actually I was hoping you could help me with something. Colonel Marsden is suffering from a painful bout of gout at the moment, and his biggest worry is that his dogs aren't being walked."

Jack's expression turned serious. He might be a bit of a joker, but he had a heart of gold. When Krish and Freddie had approached him during their crusade to ban fireworks, he had offered to help immediately.

"I thought I hadn't seen him yesterday. I can normally set my watch by him. Poor old chap. Look, I can definitely call round in the mornings and walk his dogs when I take Baxter out, but evenings might be a bit trickier—I'm usually busy here."

"Mornings would be a big help," replied Meera, gratefully. "And maybe you can think of someone who could pop in and sit with him, check he's had something to eat, that sort of thing. Hopefully, it should only be for a week or so."

"Leave it with me, Meera. I'll see what I can do," Jack assured her.

THE LAST CALL of the morning was not officially on Meera's schedule. With a slight sense of trepidation, she lifted the shiny brass knocker and tapped lightly on the door of the dower house. A few seconds later it was opened by Lady Caroline Hanley. She was an elegant, slim woman with pale blue eyes, who was rarely seen in anything other than her uniform of cashmere twinset and pearls.

"Good morning, Doctor Kumar."

"Hello," replied Meera, feeling unusually nervous. "I was

wondering if I might have a word."

After the briefest pause, Caroline nodded. "Of course. Do come in."

She led Meera through into the drawing room where a Siamese cat was snoozing in front of a blazing fire. The dower house was elegantly and expensively decorated with antique furniture, silk curtains and Persian rugs. Meera, who had always had an eye for interior design, thought it might be the most beautiful house in the village. She hoped one day to make her new home look as lovely.

"How are you all settling in at the Grange?" asked Caroline, as if reading her mind.

"We still have some work left to do, but it's starting to feel like home, thank you."

"I'm pleased. It's a house that holds many happy memories for me."

Meera thought this was an odd remark. Guy had been the previous owner of the Grange. Even before he was arrested, he and Caroline hadn't been close, but Meera didn't query her comment. Caroline was polite, but there was a coldness about her. Even when she smiled, it looked brittle. Like her face might crack, Jo would say. It was difficult to think of someone less like Lucy. Meera sensed this was the end of the small talk and decided to get to the point of her visit. She cleared her throat, not quite sure how to address such a delicate issue.

"I've also been busy making changes at the surgery," she began. "Since I took over, we have been updating the way we store our medical records. As I entered your details on to the new database, I couldn't help noticing that you had a blood test eighteen months ago. The results showed the white blood cell count was very low, but no treatment seems to have been offered. Did Dr Robertson speak to you about the results?"

"That incompetent old fool!" tutted Caroline. "I referred myself to Mr Charnsworth. He has rooms in Harley Street."

Meera nodded. Oscar Charnsworth was one of the country's leading oncologists.

"And was Mr Charnsworth able to give you a diagnosis?"

"He did. I have myeloma. There is no cure."

She delivered this news as if she were discussing the weather, without any hint of emotion. It was what Meera had feared.

"There isn't, but it is treatable. There are various options to maintain your quality of life and prolong it," she suggested gently, but Caroline interrupted her immediately.

"Be pumped so full of chemicals and feeling worse than I do now? No thank you."

"Are you in pain?"

"Nothing I can't bear."

"Are you still seeing Mr Charnsworth?"

"No, not since his diagnosis. He said I may have another five years. Three score years and ten is more than enough for anyone, Dr Kumar."

Meera decided to try another tack. "Have you spoken about this to anyone else? I'm sure Lucy would want to know."

Caroline rose to her feet. "Dr Kumar. Nobody else knows about this and I expect it to remain that way."

Meera bristled slightly. She took all her patients' confidentiality very seriously. "Of course," she said, also standing. The discussion was clearly over. "But please think about what I've said. There are a range of treatments we could try. I'd be very happy to discuss them with you at any time."

By now they were back at the front door.

"Thank you, Doctor. It was kind of you to call."

Meera knew when she was being dismissed. Reluctantly, she left the dower house, but as she walked back to the surgery she couldn't help wondering if she could have said anything that would make Caroline change her mind.

The older members of the village were still in her thoughts that evening as she cooked a lamb balti for supper, while Ben helped Krish with his homework at the kitchen table. Suddenly she heard Ben saying her name and looked over her shoulder, to see him grinning back at her.

"Ah so you are receiving us. We called your name three times. We need your help with tonight's French."

"Sorry, I was miles away. What was the question?"

Krish frowned at his book. He hated French. "Is it *il pleut* or *il fait pleut*?"

"*Il pleut*," replied Meera, who had enjoyed learning a foreign language, but had dropped it to take three sciences instead.

"What were you thinking about?" asked Ben.

"Some of my patients. I went to see the colonel this morning. His foot isn't getting any better and he's worried about his dogs not getting enough exercise."

"I could walk them for him, Mum?" offered Krish eagerly.

"Don't be silly, Krish. You're allergic to dogs."

"I'm not as bad as I used to be. I never have an asthma attack when I'm with Freddie and his dogs and I'd be outside. Please, Mum, I'd like to help. The colonel has been really nice to me. He was great at cricket coaching in the summer. He said I would make an excellent wicket keeper."

"He could ride his bike there. It would only take him about ten minutes," chimed in Ben, who had bought Krish a new bike for his birthday the previous month.

"If I go now, I could be back before it gets dark and I promise I'll finish my homework after tea," said Krish, pre-empting Meera's next argument. She sighed and raised her hands in the air. She knew she was beaten when the two of them ganged up on her like this.

"All right. You can try, but if your asthma flares up, you have to stop, okay?"

"Thanks, Mum!" he called as he disappeared out of the door.

Meera picked up her phone and dialled the colonel's number to tell him Krish was on his way. It would be nice to deliver good news for a change.

CHAPTER THREE

R ACHEL SWEPT UP the last of the soggy toilet paper from the playground and dumped it in the rubbish bin with a sigh.

"Thank God it's Friday!" she muttered. A strong gust of wind whipped the long strands of her hair that had come loose from her ponytail across her face. She shivered and reached in her pocket for a tissue. It felt like she was coming down with a cold. Her half-term trip to sunny Athens with Sarah, seemed like a long time ago. The watch strap on her wrist slipped as she tried to wipe her hands dry. Her tan was beginning to fade already. Tucking her chin into the collar of her coat, she locked the gate and hurried up the lane before it began to rain again.

"I'm home!" she called out as she stepped through the back door of her cottage.

"How was your day?" asked Sarah as Rachel shrugged off her dripping coat.

"Exhausting. We started a new topic. The ancient Egyptians. I thought I'd get them interested by asking a volunteer to be a mummy and wrapping them up in loo roll."

"What could possibly go wrong?" said Sarah with a wry smile.

"It was fine until Jared got hold of a roll and lobbed it out of the window. It rolled right across the playground, through the railings and down to the shop. Nora was not happy."

"Is she ever happy?"

"Good point. What are you up to?"

Sarah was curled up on the sofa with her laptop open on her knee.

"We finished early. It was too wet to do any proper digging, so I sent the others back to York and thought I'd do a bit of virtual digging instead."

Rachel peered over her shoulder at the screen, then froze. Looking back at her was a picture of Lord Rupert Hanley. Lucy's late husband and someone Rachel had known all her life.

"Why are you reading about Rupert?" she asked trying to keep her tone neutral as a sense of foreboding began to grow inside her.

"This morning, before the deluge, we found a cufflink. One of the students got overexcited until I pointed out it was definitely twenty-first century. I assumed it belonged to Rob as we found it on his land, and it was engraved with the initials RH. When I saw him and Lucy, I gave it to him. Lucy turned as white as a sheet. Rob explained it wasn't his but Rupert's. That got me thinking. I know on that day we were first called out that everyone thought it was his body that had been found, but I realised I didn't really know much about him and what happened."

"Nobody does. Not really," said Rachel quietly. Rupert had disappeared on the night the country first went into lockdown. Months later his remains had been found in a nearby cave. The police had stopped investigating after the coroner declared an open verdict. Only Rachel, Lucy, Jo and Meera knew that Lucy had argued with her husband on the land where Rob's house, the Hayloft, now stood. She had hit him in self-defence and when she didn't see him again, she'd been convinced she'd killed him.

"What was he like?" asked Sarah, interrupting Rachel's thoughts.

"Selfish, arrogant, cruel," she replied bluntly.

The anger in her voice made Sarah turn and give her a questioning look.

"He must have been okay at one time. Why else would Lucy have married him?"

"He could be charming when he wanted to be." Rachel shrugged. "But I guess drugs change people. Was Lucy okay?"

Sarah's bright green eyes turned cold.

"Fine, I think. I expect it's always a bit of a shock when something from your past appears unexpectedly, but she's moved on, hasn't she? Now she's got a new man in her life."

Rachel heard the edge to her voice and decided to change the subject. Ever since Sarah had discovered that Rachel had once thought of Lucy as being more than a friend, she became quite frosty whenever Rachel mentioned her best friend. It was the only point of contention in their relationship and the one thing that stopped Rachel telling Sarah everything about Rupert's disappearance.

"How about I make a risotto for supper?" she suggested, heading into the kitchen.

"Sounds wonderful!" Sarah called after her.

Rachel found her favourite pan and started rummaging through the fridge for ingredients.

"We are out of wine," she shouted without realising Sarah had followed her through. Rachel turned with a start when she felt her hand on her shoulder. "I could go to the pub and get a bottle, or shall we both go for a pre-dinner drink? I haven't seen Jack in a while."

"No you go. I'll make a start on chopping the onions and mushrooms. Don't be long," she said, dropping a kiss on Rachel's head.

FOR ONCE THE White Hart wasn't too busy. She found Jack, her oldest friend, over by the table in the window where Meera and Ben were sitting.

"Evening, Miss Foxton!" he said with a grin. "It looks like you have survived your first week back."

"Only just," replied Rachel grimly.

"Would you like to join us?" offered Meera. "Our kitchen is out of use for a couple of days while the plumbers fit a new sink and Krish is having a sleepover with Freddie, so we thought we'd treat ourselves to dinner out."

"No thanks, Meera," Rachel replied. "I've left Sarah prepping supper. I've only come to get a bottle of wine."

"Red or white?" asked Jack.

"White, please."

"I'll get it," said Jo, jumping down from the stool at the bar she was perched on. Since she and Jack had got together,

Jo spent most evenings in the pub with him, occasionally helping out if they got busy. She went behind the bar and retrieved a bottle of sauvignon blanc from the fridge.

"Thanks," said Rachel handing over the cash, then turning back to Meera. "How did Lucy seem when you saw her?"

Meera looked a little puzzled. "Fine, I think. Although I didn't really speak to her. She was ordering pizzas for Rob to collect on his way home. Why do you ask?"

Although Meera knew what had happened on the night Rupert disappeared, Rachel didn't want to bring up the whole story of the cufflink in the middle of the pub, so she simply shrugged. "No reason really. Has Rob officially moved into the Hall?"

"I think so," said Meera. "He always seems to be there, but doesn't he still own the Hayloft?"

"Yes. He wants to sell it but is going to wait until Sarah has finished the dig. He's not sure how keen people will be to buy with her team unearthing dead Druids next door, but he's been really good about it, telling Sarah to take as long as she needs."

"That is kind of him. I think he and Lucy make a lovely couple. She's so bubbly and outgoing while he's the strong, silent type. Like Mr Rochester," sighed Meera, ever the romantic.

"Surely, with Lucy being a bit posh, he'd be more of a Mellors," said Jack with a grin.

"I didn't know you were a fan of D H Lawrence, Jack," said Meera, who was an avid reader and adored all the classics.

"No need to sound so surprised! You and Ben aren't the

only intellectuals around here," said Jack, pretending to look offended as Meera flushed with embarrassment. "I'm only joking, Meera," he reassured her. "I haven't read *Lady Chatterley* properly. When I was a kid we passed it round the team bus, looking for all the dirty bits."

"I did the same," Jo said with a laugh. "I sneaked into the school library to read it because the nuns had banned it from the children's home. I was only interested in the naughty bits too."

"And what did you think?" asked Jack.

Jo shrugged. "A bit disappointing really."

Rachel laughed along with the others. It was strange. A few months ago, she wouldn't have been able to joke about Lucy being in a new relationship—it would have been too painful—but now she had Sarah and a new future to look forward to.

"I'd better go," she said. "I'm meant to be cooking."

"I'm going too," said Jo reaching for her jacket and kissing Jack goodbye. "I need to get some sleep. I feel dead on my feet."

Out on the street, Rachel waved Jo goodbye and hurried across the road, only to see Becky, her sister, walking just as quickly towards her. She checked her watch and tutted.

"I thought you started work at five?" she said loudly.

Becky stopped abruptly and scowled at her. "I'm only a few minutes late. Jack won't mind."

"That's hardly the attitude. He gave you that waitressing job as a favour to me. You shouldn't take advantage of him."

"I'm not," snapped Becky, flicking her long blonde hair away from her face. "Besides it's not my fault—the traffic from Leeds was terrible."

Rachel narrowed her eyes. "Have you been with Nish all day? Leaving Mum to look after Minty, I expect."

"She enjoys it. They both do and if I have been with Nish or if I'm late, it really is none of your business, so butt out."

With that she stomped over to the pub. Rachel watched her go. Becky and her little girl now lived with Mary, their mother, in the old family farmhouse. Max, her soon to be ex-husband, was on remand awaiting trial. He had used his position as Lucy's estate manager to steal from her and tried to do the same to Mary. After running away to Spain, he had finally been caught when Rachel found him hiding out in a deserted farmhouse. Automatically, her hand went to touch the scar on her forehead from where he'd hit her.

Becky had always sworn she had no idea what he was up to. More than anything, Rachel wanted to believe that her selfish little sister wasn't guilty of anything more than being naïve, but like a chameleon, since meeting Meera's brother, Nish, she had transformed from being the wife of a would-be country squire to girlfriend of a cool city clubber. Sometimes she wondered if Becky had a mind of her own. A few heavy raindrops began to fall, and Rachel sneezed twice. She was definitely coming down with a cold. Pushing all thoughts of Becky to one side, she dashed back to Sarah and the warmth of the cottage.

"HOW MUCH DO you think Rob will want for the Hayloft,

when he puts it on the market?" asked Sarah as Rachel spooned the risotto on to their plates and Sarah poured the wine.

"No idea. A lot I should imagine. Why, are you planning on moving?"

Sarah smiled. "No, but I thought it would make a great home for the heritage centre. You know, as it's right next to the burial ground."

The idea of creating a centre for the study of Celtic history in Hartwell was something the two women were passionate about. Even before she arrived in Hartwell, Sarah had been studying the work of Joseph Baxter Tarrant, a young archaeologist who was buried in Hartwell's churchyard. He had been writing a paper on the legend of the Hartwell nobles. These were a collection of ancient silver coins belonging to the Foxtons and the other families who had always lived in the village. One of the Hanley's ancestors had given them away in attempt to lift a Druid curse for building Hartwell Hall on sacred land. However, the villagers were tricked as the coins turned out to be silver instead of the promised gold and the Hanley men were still said to be cursed. This story, combined with all the artefacts Sarah and her team had found, had convinced them Hartwell should have a Celtic heritage centre. Now all they needed to do was find the right place to house it.

AFTER SUPPER, RACHEL had a long soak in a hot bath and went to bed early in the hope of fending off the cold while

Sarah stayed downstairs looking into funding for heritage sites. As Rachel pulled the duvet up to her ears and closed her eyes, she could hear the occasional whirl of the printer.

It would be wonderful for the two of them to work together on a project. She only hoped Sarah's sudden interest in Rupert would be short-lived.

CHAPTER FOUR

J O LEANED HER head back against the cool bathroom tiles and groaned. She closed her eyes and slowly inhaled, before another wave of nausea hit. Her stomach heaved and she wretched into the toilet bowl.

"Oh, please stop," she moaned, wiping her mouth. She had been slumped here for the last hour. Whenever she tried to move, she threw up again. It had been the same yesterday. Foolishly, she'd starved herself for twenty-four hours, thinking she might have food poisoning. However, the little white stick with the two blue lines lying on the floor next to her, told her differently. While she waited for her stomach to settle, she racked her brains to think when she'd last had her period. She'd never been very regular and didn't bother to keep track.

She retched again. How could this have happened? Then it came to her. The weekend in London. Jack had taken her down there as a surprise for her birthday. He'd made her wear a blindfold in the car and refused to tell her where they were going until they hit the M25.

"You're always complaining about how much you miss the place," he'd said and laughed at her stunned face.

It was the first time back in her home city since she'd

been sent to Hartwell. She'd only been away a few months, but it had still felt weird. Playing at being a tourist. They had stayed in a lovely boutique hotel in Covent Garden, gone to a show in the West End and taken a boat trip on the Thames. Jack had spent a small fortune in Fortnum and Mason buying food and wine so they could have a picnic in St James's Park. It was there, behind an oak tree in one of the Royal Parks that passion had taken over. She remembered giggling that if one of her old colleagues caught them, they'd be arrested. As it turned out the risk of arrest wasn't the biggest consequence of their recklessness.

Her birthday had been in early September. So how many weeks did that make. Eight? Maybe more. She counted on her fingers. That could mean the baby would be here in May, maybe June, she wasn't sure. A baby! Oh God! She and Jack wouldn't even have been together a year. She groaned again. Oh, Jack! How was he going to handle this? She took another deep breath and finally the sickness began to subside. Slowly, she staggered to her feet. She could only deal with one problem at a time and constantly throwing up was the most immediate one. Thankfully, she had a couple of days off, but tomorrow she was due at work. She'd never make it if she felt this bad.

AN HOUR LATER, she was standing in the pregnancy and baby aisle of the chemist's in Thirsk and realised she was totally out of her depth. She'd hoped to grab some pills promising to cure morning sickness, but instead she was faced with a confusing array of supplements, vitamins and ointments. The creams for stretch marks and cracked nipples made her wince and she began to feel light-headed again.

She needed to speak to an expert. Pushing her way past the other customers and the staff in white coats, she hurried back outside.

MEERA ANSWERED THE door of the Grange with a polite smile, but her smile quickly faded when she saw Jo.

"Oh, my goodness! You look terrible. Come in, come in. What's wrong?"

"I'm pregnant," Jo blurted out, as Meera closed the door behind her.

"Oh, my goodness," repeated Meera more loudly. She looked as stunned as Jo felt.

"Shush," said Jo, raising her fingers to her lips. She could see Ben and Krish sitting at the kitchen table. Telling Meera was one thing, but she wasn't sure she wanted her news to become public knowledge yet.

"Sorry," whispered Meera. "Follow me into my study."

Meera's study was a small room off the hallway, painted pale yellow with curtains covered in a daffodil print. It was every bit as neat and tidy as Jo would have expected. Meera ushered her inside and sat her down on the armchair by the window while she settled into the chair at her desk.

"I'm really sorry to bother you at home. I know I should have made an appointment at the surgery, but I took a test this morning and, well, I panicked," Jo said, her words tumbling out.

"Don't be silly. It wasn't so long ago I phoned you in the middle of the night in a total panic and you came over without a second thought."

Jo smiled weakly at the memory. Dealing with a possible kidnapper had been far simpler than her current predicament. Meera peered over her glasses and fixed her dark eyes on Jo.

"I take it this wasn't planned?"

Jo shook her head.

"How many weeks along are you?"

Jo shrugged. Meera had switched from friend to doctor mode very quickly and suddenly everything was beginning to feel very real.

"Eight, I think. I've never really kept track of that kind of thing."

Meera shifted in her seat. "I see." She paused. "And are you planning on keeping the baby?"

Jo stared back at her. It was the most obvious question in the circumstances, but it wasn't until she heard her friend ask it out loud that Jo knew the answer. There was a little life growing inside, depending on her. She wouldn't let it down.

"Yes," she said fiercely, "I am not getting rid of it, now or later. I'm going to do a better job than my own mother did."

Meera reached over and squeezed her hand. "I'm sorry, I wasn't sure if that was the reason you were here. You've never mentioned having children or seemed very keen on them, if I'm being completely honest."

"I'm not," agreed Jo. "I mean I like Krish and Freddie, but generally I find them pretty annoying."

Meera sat back and looked business-like again. "Are you still eating that awful, sugary breakfast cereal every morning?"

"Yes, why?"

"Because the one good thing it does contain is folic acid. I take it you haven't been taking any dietary supplements?"

"No."

"You really need to start taking better care of yourself, Jo."

"I'm perfectly healthy," she protested weakly.

"You are, but quite frankly that's a miracle considering your diet and lifestyle. I don't think I've ever known you to have your recommended five a day. You need to increase your intake of fruits and vegetables and consider taking a supplement for expectant mums."

"Okay," agreed Jo, quietly. "Expectant mum. That sounds so weird."

"You'll have to stop drinking too. How many units have you had over the last few weeks?"

"I didn't think doctors were meant to be this judgemental."

Meera folded her arms and gave her a stern look. "This doctor also happens to be speaking as a friend who knows all your bad habits. How many units?"

"Hardly any. I've either been too tired or felt too ill."

"Good. You're going to have to give up smoking too."

"I know, I know." Jo sighed, rolling up her sleeve to reveal her arm covered in the nicotine patches she'd bought along with the pregnancy test. "Is there anything you can give me to stop the sickness? I spent the whole morning with my head stuck down the loo."

"You should take vitamin B-6 and ginger tea is meant to be very good."

Jo pulled a face.

"It's only early days yet," Meera reassured her. "If it doesn't improve, I'll write you a prescription."

Meera opened her desk drawer and produced a handful of leaflets. "When you are ready there are lots of childbirth support and antenatal groups you can join."

Jo looked at her in horror and held up her hands. "No way. Thanks, Meera, but I'm really not a support group kind of person. All that sitting around in a circle, talking about my feelings." She gave a shudder. "I'll manage on my own." She paused. "Maybe with your help too."

"What about Jack? Have you told him yet?"

Jo shook her head. "No. He's been away for the weekend. An old rugby friend's stag do."

At that moment, her phone bleeped. She looked at the screen and smiled. "Speak of the devil. He should be home in an hour."

BACK AT HER cottage, Jo sat watching the hands of the wall clock tick around while she nibbled on a ginger biscuit Meera had packed her off with. She was used to breaking bad news. Telling a distraught husband his beautiful wife had been killed in a traffic collision or a disbelieving mother that her adored son had been caught dealing drugs, but this was uncharted territory. She had no idea how Jack would react.

They'd only been together a few months. Having children was something she had never thought about let alone discussed with a boyfriend.

One thing she did know now, was that whatever his reaction she was keeping her baby. As soon as Meera had asked her, she'd felt an overwhelming wave of protectiveness for the tiny life growing inside her. He or she was relying on Jo, and she wasn't going to let them down. Her thoughts drifted to her own mother. She must have known she wouldn't be able to keep her, yet she'd still gone through the pregnancy. Jo had been abandoned as a baby when she was only a few hours old. All she'd been left with was a note, saying her name was Jo, and one of the Hartwell nobles, the ancient coins that most of the village families had. Why? What was her mother thinking? The bleeping of her phone interrupted her thoughts. Jack was home.

The pub wasn't open yet, but she found him in the bar glugging down a bottle of fruit juice.

"Dehydrated?" she queried.

"A bit," he replied, grinning as he stepped forward and hugged her, "I must be out of practice. I feel really rough." He stepped back and surveyed her. "You look worse though. What's up?"

Jo took a deep breath and decided not to sugar-coat her news. "I'm pregnant," she said bluntly.

Jack stared at her silently for a few seconds, then his face broke into a huge grin. He lifted her off her feet and twirled her round as she protested loudly. Then he set her carefully down and lowered himself to the floor, wincing slightly as he rested on his one good knee.

"Will you marry, me. I'm sorry I haven't got a ring—this is a bit of a surprise."

Jo put her hand on her hips and tutted in exasperation. "Get up. We are not getting married just because I'm pregnant. I can only handle one drama at a time. We need to decide what we're doing about the baby."

Jack staggered to his feet, his face turning pale. "What do you mean? Don't you want it? Because I do, Jo, I really do. I know it's your choice and everything." He was beginning to stammer and Jo put her hand on his arm.

"I'm not saying that. I do want it. I'm saying this wasn't planned. Both our lives are going to change. Whatever happens between us as a couple, we'll always have a child together. We wouldn't be able to please ourselves anymore. Already I feel so rotten, I don't think I'll be up to working tomorrow and it'll probably wreck any hope I had of getting back to Scotland Yard."

"It won't wreck your career," protested Jack. "You'll only be out of action for a few months. There's no reason for you not being able to move back to London still. I keep telling you the Met will want you back as soon as they see sense."

"And then what? You can hardly run the White Hart from Hackney."

"We could all move to London. You, me and the baby. I could take care of it while you were working. I've got a few mates who own pubs down there. One of them would give me a job even if it was only part-time. We had a great time when we were there for your birthday."

"A weekend staying in a flash hotel and cruising the Thames isn't the same as living there," huffed Jo.

Jack pulled her gently towards him and wrapped his arms tightly around her. "I know that, but it doesn't mean we can't make it work if we want to," he said. He placed a kiss on top of her head and Jo leaned into him. Suddenly she felt very tired again.

"I'm being a miserable cow, aren't I?" she said, her voice muffled against his chest.

"But you are my beautiful miserable cow and I love you very much and I'll love our baby too."

Jo raised her head. "I love you too, but I'm still going to blame you when I get swollen ankles and stretch marks."

"I wouldn't have it any other way."

AS PREDICTED, THE next day she didn't make it into work. For the first time in her life, she called in sick. It was lunchtime before she left the bathroom. Jack, who had spent most of the morning anxiously waiting outside the door, insisted on her coming back to the White Hart, so he could keep an eye on her. So, wearing his biggest winter coat, she sat at a quiet table in the beer garden, making the most of the late autumn sun as she sipped a mineral water. She closed her eyes and wondered about the chances of having a nap without Jack or his mother disturbing her.

Shirley had actually burst into tears when they'd told her the previous evening and she'd hugged Jo so hard, she'd been in danger of cracking a rib. It had felt quite surreal. Jo wasn't used to all this love and affection.

A shadow fell across the table as Rachel slipped into the

seat next to her.

"Congratulations," she whispered softly.

Jo turned to her and raised an eyebrow. "I take it Jack told you?"

Rachel smiled and shrugged. "He's useless at keeping secrets at the best of times and he's very excited. As soon as I saw him with that daft grin on his face, I knew something was up. Don't worry though, I won't tell anyone if you don't want me to, not even Sarah."

Jo shook her head. "I don't suppose it really matters. Between him and Shirley the whole village will know by the end of the week."

"What's wrong? You don't look very happy."

"I am but it's a lot to take in and I'm stressing about what it might mean for my career." Her phone bleeped and Jo rolled her eyes and sighed as she read the message. "And I keep getting texts from Meera. It must be, like, ten so far today already. She's remembered my blood group is O negative, so apparently, I need some injections or something. She's emailing me the info along with about a hundred articles she thinks I should read." Jo wrapped her arms tightly around herself. "I really hate having injections and blood tests," she grumbled.

Rachel reached over and patted her leg. "They aren't a big deal. It's in case the baby has a positive blood group. Mum is O neg—she had to have them too when she was expecting me and Becky."

"How come everyone knows more about being pregnant and having babies than me?"

Rachel smiled, then gave her a quizzical look. "To be

honest, I never really thought motherhood was on your radar."

"Me neither, but here we are."

"I know we haven't always seen eye to eye, but for what it's worth I think you'll make a great mum."

"Thanks, Rach!"

The two of them sat in silence for a moment, before Rachel gave her a sidelong glance.

"Make sure you remember this conversation when it comes to choosing godmothers, okay?"

Jo snorted with laughter. She'd forgotten how competitive Rachel could be.

Rachel grinned. "I'm serious! I'm Jack's oldest friend, so I'm not prepared to lose out to Meera's superior medical knowledge or Lucy because she'll look better on the christening photos. And even if they are both better on the whole giving parental advice thing, remember, your childless friend will be the most reliable babysitter."

"Okay, okay. If, there is a christening, you can be godmother."

"Can I have it in writing?"

"Stop!" Jo laughed, giving her an affectionate slap.

"That's better," declared Rachel, rising to her feet. "My job here is done. You were looking far too miserable when I found you."

THAT NIGHT WHEN Jack had finished work, he and Baxter returned to Jo's cottage and found her already snuggled under the duvet. The black Labrador immediately leapt on to the bed and settled by her feet.

"How are you feeling? Did you manage to get some rest this afternoon?" he asked as he climbed in beside her and pulled her close.

"A bit," she replied sleepily, "in between visitors. First the new curate arrived—her name's Belinda. She said the rev had heard our 'happy news' and had sent her to offer his congratulations and tell us we are in his prayers. Then Lucy arrived with a recipe for ginger and honey tea from Joan along with about half of Kew Gardens."

"Ah ha!" chuckled Jack. "I did wonder where all the flowers had come from. I take it she was excited."

"You could say that. You know Lucy. There was a lot of squealing and hugging."

Jack gently stroked her hair. "Are you coping with all the attention?"

"It feels a bit weird," she admitted with a yawn, "but I guess it's nice that everyone is so happy for us."

She laced her fingers through his and, resting both their hands over her stomach, drifted off to sleep to the sound of Baxter snoring.

CHAPTER FIVE

LUCY HAD A long list of people she needed to telephone. There was the location manager for the film company, two wedding planners and the owner of a marquee hire company, but the first number she called was the Rosemary Centre. The Rosemary Centre was the area's only refuge for victims of domestic violence. Lucy had helped them with a fundraising event in the summer. It had been her and Rob's first official date.

Alison, the director of the centre, had left her a message the previous day and had sounded quite agitated. She didn't sound much calmer when she answered Lucy's call. She quickly explained that they had been dealt a double blow. Not only had their landlord refused to renew their lease, but they had also learnt that their funding from central government had been withdrawn and it looked like they may be forced to merge with a refuge in York or Leeds.

"That's terrible! What can I do to help?" asked Lucy immediately.

"Raise awareness. Write letters to the papers. Support us on social media. But what we really need is political support to get the government to reverse its decision."

"How on earth do we get that? We don't even have a

working MP at the moment."

"That might work in our favour. All the candidates will be chasing votes. If we can get them all to support us it could make a real difference. I went to a hustings in Thirsk last night and asked them about it, but they all brushed me off. I couldn't get a firm commitment from any of them."

Lucy peered at the calendar above her desk. "There's another hustings in Hartwell tonight. Why don't I go along and try again?"

"Would you?" asked Alison sounding relieved. "That would be fantastic. The more people who ask the better, especially someone who isn't directly involved. One of the candidates tried to imply I was only interested in protecting my own job."

"Cheeky sod!" exclaimed Lucy, who knew how committed Alison was to the centre. "Leave it with me. I'll report back tomorrow."

Unfortunately, she didn't have time to give the Rosemary Centre much more thought. The location manager from the film company who were making the Jane Austen adaptation was due any minute. Although most of the filming would take part in the spring, they wanted to shoot some interior scenes in January, but the Hall would need some work before then to make it look right for the Georgian period. She hurried downstairs and out of the front door, ready to greet him when he arrived. Standing on the steps beneath the portico, she waved to Bill who was hard at work.

"Don't you worry, Lady H. I'll have the place looking shipshape for them film people," he shouted above the noise of his new petrol leaf blower. He had been over the moon when Lucy had bought it for him, along with a sit-on mower.

"All right, Lucy."

She turned around at the sound of her name and saw Nish, Meera's brother, heading across the lawn to her.

"Oh hi, Nish. How are you?"

"Good thanks. I'm giving my mate a hand setting up. He's DJing at the wedding reception here tonight," he replied pointing behind him to the large marquee that had been erected the day before.

"Really? Is he any good?"

"Amazing. He's got a residency in the biggest club in Leeds. Actually, I told him I'd ask you a favour. We're parked near a big old building on the other side of the courtyard. It's got loads of broken windows and looks kind of derelict."

"The coach house?" suggested Lucy, although in truth that description could apply to most of the Hall's outbuildings.

"Yeh, that's it. If he gives you a grand would you let him use it to shoot a music video? He's releasing his first single in the new year."

"He wants to give me a thousand pounds to use the coach house?" asked Lucy incredulously.

"Yeh, is that enough? We found somewhere in Bradford but the council owned it and wouldn't give us permission. It will probably only be for the morning."

"Nish, for a grand he can have it all day," replied Lucy holding out her hand to shake on the deal as the location manager's car pulled up in front of them. It really was astonishing how the money was rolling in these days.

"I STILL DON'T know why you won't let me pay to have all the ballroom windows replaced. You can pay me back when you're ready," said Rob shrugging off his coat and unwinding the scarf from around his neck. He'd been down to London on business. When he'd arrived home half an hour ago, he offered to take her to the pub for lunch, so they could catch up.

"No," said Lucy firmly as she took a seat next to the open fire in the White Hart, "it's really kind of you and I don't mean to sound ungrateful, but it's important to me that the estate can pay for itself. I've got three weddings already booked for spring. Some of the profits from those can be used to replace the most rotten ones and I'll have to do the rest in the summer. In the meantime, the film company will do enough superficial work to make it look presentable enough for the scenes they want to shoot. So, thank you, but no."

"Fair enough," replied Rob, holding up his hands in surrender. "If you want to be self-sufficient that's fine. Am I still allowed to get you a gin and tonic?"

"Yes, please."

She watched him as he made his way to the bar. Although he'd only been away for a couple of days, she'd missed him terribly. So much it had surprised her. She and Freddie had lived on their own for such a long time before he came along, it was quite a shock to find how used she'd become to his solid, quiet presence at the kitchen table, his arm resting on her shoulder while they watched a film, and the bed had felt horribly cold and empty. He returned with their drinks. She raised her glass.

"Welcome home," she said. "It feels like you've been gone forever."

"Thanks," he replied, giving her a quizzical look as they clinked glasses. "So, it sounds like things are progressing well with the film company. What else has been happening?"

Lucy took a sip of her drink and sighed. She should have known better than to try to get him to say something romantic in the middle of the pub. It looked like it was back to business.

"Actually, there is something I wanted to run by you. The Rosemary Centre is being kicked out of their premises by their landlord and I really want to help them. I was thinking of offering them either Moorhead Farm or Netherby Heights." She paused. "Rent-free. Do you think that's a stupid idea?"

Rob shook his head thoughtfully. "Not at all. They've both been derelict for ages. You might have to charge them a token rent, say a pound a year or something, to keep the lawyers happy, but it would make sense. It's better to have a tenant renovating and maintaining the place rather than have it stood empty."

"It still doesn't help them to find funding to do all the work or with the day-to-day running costs. I was speaking with Alison earlier. She said they have lost the funding from central government. She's hoping when the new MP is elected, they'll help fight for it to be reinstated."

"I don't like her chances. I bet the candidates haven't even heard about the place."

"Oh don't say that! Actually, there's a hustings tonight at the village hall. I thought I might go along. Do you want to come too?"

Rob grimaced. "I really don't."

"Where's your sense of civic duty?" she teased.

"How about you go and report back and I'll keep Freddie company. I called in at the Natural History Museum while I was in Kensington and got him some dinosaur stuff from the gift shop. I'll get us fish and chips for tea, and we can have a boys' night."

"He'll love that. He's missed you."

Rob leaned forward and fixed those deep blue eyes on her.

"I missed him too. Almost as much as I missed you," he said softly, and Lucy was very tempted to suggest they forget lunch altogether and go straight back home. The moment was spoiled though by the sudden, noisy arrival of Ben, who manged to both hit his head on a beam and walk into a bar stool as he entered the pub.

"Hi, Ben, how are you?" asked Rob.

"Good thanks," replied the notoriously clumsy vet as he rubbed his shin.

"Time for a pint?" offered Rob, but Ben shook his head.

"No thanks. I'm working. I only called in to check on Baxter. Jack said he was off his food."

"Is he okay?" asked Lucy. Baxter was one of Tillly's puppies from a litter she'd had that spring.

"He will be. It turns out he's been raiding the bins

again," explained Ben. "He must have eaten something that disagreed with him. I've given him something to help clear it up, but he's crying outside now. Shirley has banished him to the yard. I don't think she was too keen on dog diarrhoea all over the kitchen."

Lucy felt very relieved their lunch hadn't arrived yet. Ben was lovely, but he'd never really mastered the art of small talk. Occasionally his blunt honesty could be a little unsettling. Perhaps that's why he and Meera worked so well together. She always seemed to know the perfect thing to say.

"How are the wedding plans going?" she asked, to quickly change the subject.

"Not great. We're struggling to find a venue. Meera wanted to get married at the Grange, but it turns out we can't get a licence. She's getting a bit stressed."

"I'm sorry. I'll try to think of something," said Lucy knowing Meera was capable of worrying for England and how desperate her friend was for the perfect wedding. Ben looked grateful.

"Thanks, Lucy, that would be great. Maybe you could go and have a chat with her sometime. I'm not sure I've been that helpful to be honest."

LUCY MANAGED TO persuade Meera, Rachel and even Jo to join her at the hustings in the village hall that evening.

"You look much better than when I last saw you," she said as Jo slid into the seat next to her.

"I feel better," replied Jo. "Jack made some of the tea

from Joan's recipe. It was like a magic potion. Are you sure she isn't a witch and not a housekeeper?"

"No." Lucy laughed. "But she did used to be a nurse." Next to them, Rachel flicked through all the campaign leaflets that had been handed to her on the way in and tutted.

"None of the candidates from the three main parties are from round here," she grumbled. "In fact, I bet they hadn't even set foot in North Yorkshire until the by-election was announced."

"It doesn't mean they won't do a good job," said Meera reasonably. Up on the stage three earnest-looking men in suits were chatting to the returning officer, who was in charge of the proceedings. They were indistinguishable except for the different-coloured rosettes they wore.

"I know him," said Jo pointing to the man on the right of the stage who belonged to the same party as Guy. That party had held the seat for over a hundred years, so it was almost certain he would win. "His name is Sebastian Devizes. He's a government special adviser or private secretary or something. He was always turning up at the station during the Guy investigation."

"Is he nice?" asked Meera hopefully, but Jo shook her head.

"No, he's a real creep. He said he was there to assist us, but all he did was interfere. In fact, I'd put money on him being the one who removed all the incriminating evidence from the Grange before we got a search warrant."

Lucy gave a little shudder as she recalled that some of the few items Jo did find were photos of her and Rupert arguing on the night he disappeared.

"Who's that?" asked Meera, pointing to the only female on the stage. She had long grey hair and was dressed casually in jeans and a jumper. She was sitting apart from the other candidates and looked far more nervous.

"That must be Heather Rhodes, the independent candidate," replied Lucy.

Rachel squinted at the woman and then looked at her campaign leaflet. "Oh my God!" she exclaimed. "It's my old geography teacher. I haven't seen her in years."

"What's she like?" asked Meera.

"She was a great teacher. Really into being green before it was fashionable. Some of the kids used to call her Heather the Hippy. She was studying for a PhD. I wonder what made her want to change from being an academic to a politician."

"Money probably," replied Jo, who was slowly working her way through a large bag of Maltesers much to Meera's disapproval. "Speaking of academics, where's Sarah? I thought this sort of thing would be right up her street?"

"She's at home. She's preparing for the presentation to the parish council, so we can get their backing for Hartwell's Celtic history centre. We need to show we have local support," explained Rachel, without adding that Sarah tended to avoid any event that involved Lucy.

At that moment, the returning officer rose to his feet and the meeting began. Each candidate made an opening speech. Heather Rhodes was up first. Her voice had a slight quiver, but she spoke passionately about how much she loved the Yorkshire countryside and how protecting it was at the heart of her campaign. The next candidate declared his campaign was about policies and not personalities, which was lucky as he didn't seem to have one. He was followed by the candidate for the main opposition party, who angrily criticised the government and everything it stood for. Seb Devizes was by far the most polished public speaker. He confidently listed all his party's achievements and declared that they were the only party who continued to support 'the hardworking families of Hartwell'.

"Well, so far Heather the Hippy gets my vote," whispered Jo.

"Mine too, but I bet he still gets in," replied Rachel as Seb Devizes sat down to polite applause.

After the speeches, the floor was opened up to questions from the audience. One of Rachel's many uncles stood up and asked about farming subsidies. Nora demanded to know what they would do to help small businesses, and then it was Lucy's turn. She stood up and spoke in her clearest voice.

"The Rosemary Centre is the only charity in this constituency dedicated to supporting victims of domestic violence, yet their funding has been withdrawn and they may soon be homeless. May I ask each candidate to promise, if they are elected, to support this important charity and make reinstating its funding their number-one priority."

All four candidates nodded earnestly. The dull young man told her that he empathised deeply and asked Lucy to forward all the details to him at his campaign headquarters so he could review the situation. His angry neighbour declared that this was yet another example of the government's vicious cuts to public spending without saying what he would do about it. Then it was Devizes's turn.

"My party has an excellent track record when it comes to putting women's safety at the very forefront of their policies," he replied smoothly.

"If that was the case we wouldn't be here," heckled Rachel. "Or are you hoping we've forgotten about Guy Lovell?"

His smile turned icy and Lucy was suddenly reminded of Rupert. Devizes was wearing the exact expression her late husband had worn, usually before he delivered a particularly cruel put-down or insult.

"As I'm sure you are aware, it would be inappropriate for me to comment on that particular case while legal proceedings are still ongoing," he said. His cold eyes fixed on Rachel as if daring her to speak again, but it was Lucy who stood up once more. She might not like the man, but Rachel was right—it was almost certain he would win. She needed him on side.

"All I'm asking you to do is campaign for the funding to be reinstated. The Rosemary Centre is so important to the local community. Without it, women needing to escape dangerous situations will have to go to Hull or Leeds, miles away from friends and family. It really isn't such a huge amount in the big scheme of things."

"I'm not sure you understand the many demands on the public purse, Lady Hanley," replied Devizes, emphasising her title. He was trying to make it look like she was out of touch, when in reality she knew better than most what it felt like to be frightened in your own home.

"And perhaps you don't understand how important the safety of victims of domestic violence is to this community." She turned to the only woman on the panel. "Dr Rhodes, can the Rosemary Centre count on your support?"

Heather Rhodes turned a deep shade of red. "I'm ashamed to say that until the previous hustings I was unaware of the Rosemary Centre." She paused and looked apologetic. "I'm sure they do sterling work, but I won't promise something I can't deliver and as I've said my priorities for this constituency are education and the environment."

Lucy felt her shoulders slump.

"I commend Dr Rhodes for her honesty," said Devizes swiftly. He was clearly delighted that the female candidate hadn't forced him to publicly criticise a decision made by his own government.

"Huh! Patronising much!" muttered Jo through a mouthful of chocolate. "Don't say we're going to be saddled with this condescending sod!"

"Mr Devizes, your party is almost certain to retain this seat. If I were lucky enough to represent this lovely community in Westminster, I would make representing the most vulnerable my priority," continued Lucy, hating the sound of the falter in her voice.

"Then it's a shame you aren't standing, Lady Hanley," replied Devizes sounding very pleased with himself.

Something inside Lucy snapped. "Well as from now, I am," she retorted. She turned to the returning officer who had been busy checking his phone. "If nobody else will stand up for the most vulnerable women in this constituency, I will. I want my name added to the ballot paper."

The room erupted in noisy chatter. The photographer from the local paper leapt to his feet to capture the moment and the four candidates on the stage looked stunned.

"Luce, what are you doing?" hissed Rachel.

"Oh my goodness," murmured Meera.

The meeting finished and, amid much noise and chatter, Lucy marched up to the returning officer to collect the necessary forms, avoiding making eye contact with the other candidates. As she tried to leave, she found her way blocked by the local press, who wanted a quote and a photograph. When she finally escaped, she found her three friends waiting outside.

"Lucy, what have you done! You do realise that if you hand those forms back in, your name will appear on the ballot paper," said Rachel.

Lucy shrugged her shoulders. "I know, I know, but I felt I had to do something. That awful man was so pompous and condescending."

"I thought you were very brave," Meera reassured her with a smile.

"I think you've lost your mind," said Jo.

"Jo, that's not very supportive," Meera chided her, but Jo as usual was unrepentant.

"I'm serious. Politics is a dirty business. Do you really want to give your opponents and the press an excuse to go raking through your past? And if you win…" she continued.

"I won't win, Jo," insisted Lucy. "I just wanted to draw attention to the lack of funding for the Rosemary Centre. If I make enough noise, then the other candidates will have to promise to support the place too and I won't be needed."

It seemed quite simple to her, she couldn't understand why her friends looked so worried.

"Actually, I think you've got a decent chance," said Rachel. "I wouldn't vote for any of those muppets from the three main parties. Not one of them is from around here. How can they know what is important to us? And as much as I like Heather, she wasn't really connecting with the audience."

Jo pointed directly at Lucy. "You see. It's quite possible you'll get elected. Then what? Westminster is full of men who'll make Rupert and Guy look like a pair of kittens. I really don't think you know what you've let yourself in for."

"Why don't we all go for a drink and talk about it calmly," suggested Meera setting off down the lane.

"Great, I can't even have a proper drink," complained Jo trudging after her.

Rachel took Lucy's arm as they followed the other two up to the White Hart. "If you do get elected, I want you to make it a law that Jo never has to give up booze again," she whispered. "It makes her far too bloody grumpy."

WHEN LUCY FINALLY returned to Hartwell Hall, she found Freddie tucked up in bed with Root and Pickle sleeping at his feet. Downstairs, Rob and Tilly were slumped together on the sofa, both snoring gently. Lucy bent her head and placed a kiss gently on his lips. Slowly he opened his eyes with a smile, then reached up and pulled her on to his lap. She curled up against him, careful not to wake up the still-snoozing Labrador.

"Interesting night?" Rob murmured into her hair, sounding half asleep.

"You could say that. I said I would stand in the election too."

Suddenly Rob's eyes were wide open. "What? Why?"

"I know it sounds a bit mad, but none of the other candidates would commit to fully supporting the Rosemary Centre, and this one guy, Devizes, was really patronising, so I felt I had to do something."

"What did your friends say?"

"Meera was very supportive and Rachel said she understood why I did it."

"And Jo?"

"Actually, she was a bit negative. She basically said the House of Commons would be a nest of vipers full of men like Guy and Rupert."

Rob nodded slowly. "She might have a point."

Lucy felt a pang. She knew she'd been impetuous, but she'd really hoped she could count on Rob's support. "You don't think I should stand."

"I'm not saying that, but you can't get away from the fact that even after two female prime ministers, politics is still dominated by men. I'd say the same is still true about the police. Jo must have had to fight to get to be a DS in the Met and take a lot of crap too."

"And Jo is much tougher than me," said Lucy, quietly finishing his sentence.

"I don't want to see you get hurt," he said gently. "You hid yourself away from the gossip and the press when Rupert was found and Guy was arrested. By doing this you are inviting them into your life."

"I know I am, but I felt like I had to do something. Something dramatic to make the main party candidates take the Rosemary Centre seriously. The women there are scared and frightened, like I was. They want a safe place too, but they aren't as lucky as me—they don't have a huge mansion to hide away in." Rob pulled her close and stroked her hair. "You know what else?" she said.

"What?" he asked.

"I am so tired of being scared."

"Then I'm behind you one hundred per cent. Whatever you need, you've got it."

"You mean that?"

"One hundred per cent."

"I thought you weren't interested in politics."

"I'm not, but I am interested in you."

CHAPTER SIX

M EERA SAT BY the open fire sipping a cup of green tea
in the newly decorated drawing room. It had been a
week since Mr Linter had finished working in there. A faint
smell of paint was still in the air and several framed pencil
drawings of the local area were stacked on the floor, waiting
to be hung on the walls. There were a million jobs she
should be getting on with, but she wanted to take a moment
to sit and think.

Since Jo's visit, she'd felt unsettled. She was thrilled for
her friend, but her news had made her face something that
she had been trying not to think about. The fact she wasn't
pregnant herself. Unlike Jo, she'd religiously been taking the
correct amount of vitamins and minerals, but it had been
over three months now. If she were talking to a patient, she
would say that three months isn't very long at all, but she
couldn't help comparing her current situation to the only
other time she'd been pregnant. It seemed a little unfair—her
one and only encounter with Dev had resulted in Krish, and
yet now she'd found a man she was madly in love with and
who wanted to spend the rest of his life with her. Nothing.

Perhaps it was fate, nature's way of telling her she was
moving too quickly. It was less than a year since she'd moved

to Hartwell and met Ben. Now they were living together and planning to marry and spend their first Christmas together. It had been a whirlwind and when she stopped to think about it, she began to panic, but for ten years she'd been living a half-life—working, looking after Krish and pretending to the rest of the world there was nothing wrong with her marriage. Finding Ben, she'd suddenly felt like she had a chance to really live again, and she had grabbed it with both hands.

Pinned to the noticeboard in the kitchen was the latest postcard from Dev. He was still in Australia with his boyfriend and a scribbled note on the back of a picture of a kangaroo or koala was the only contact he'd had with his son. Krish seemed fine about it, but Meera couldn't help feeling sorry for him. Thankfully, Dev's lack of communication hadn't impeded the divorce proceedings. He'd signed all the forms and even agreed to Meera having sole custody of their son. The decree nisi had been granted and in a matter of weeks so would the decree absolute.

Everything had gone remarkably smoothly except for an irate telephone call from her soon-to-be ex-father-in-law. Dev's father was extremely wealthy and extremely unpleasant. She strongly suspected the reason for Dev remaining on the other side of the world was to avoid his bullying. Not being able to contact his son, he had instead ranted and raved down the line at Meera. He called her ungrateful after all the money he'd spent on her wedding and buying her and Dev a home. He told her she was a bad wife and mother to divorce his son. He declared she and Krish would never see another penny of his money.

Meera had calmly told him that she was divorcing his son and marrying another man and never wanted to hear from him again. Then she had done something she'd never done before. She put the phone down on him.

Meera sighed and went to the window. She had enough on her mind without recalling that particular conversation. Her wedding to Ben was something else that was giving her a headache. He had proposed in this very room with all their friends and family nearby. It had been so romantic. He'd dressed up in a period costume borrowed from a film company who were shooting an adaptation of *Jane Eyre* at Hartwell Hall. Meera had decided the theme of the wedding would have a similar period drama feeling. Candlelight, violin quartet, her dress inspired by her favourite Jane Austen characters.

The only problem was the venue. Initially, Meera had wanted them to get married here at the Grange, their new house, but private homes could not be granted a civil ceremony licence. They could get married in a church or registry office, then hold the party at the Grange. But that had led to more problems. Due to her religion, the village church was out, and the nearest registry office was in Thirsk and was not very large.

This had led to a discussion about the number of guests they would invite. Having had a huge wedding with several hundred people, many flying in from India, when she'd married Dev, this time Meera wanted something more intimate. Immediate family and their friends from the village was what she and Ben had decided on, in essence the people who had been present at the proposal, but her mother was horrified at the idea of her sisters and their families not being invited.

"Shall we elope to Gretna Green?" Ben had whispered into her ear as they'd cuddled up in bed one night, after a particularly tense conversation with her parents. He was only half joking. Meera had to admit the idea was very tempting, but her parents would never forgive her. She'd kept them in the dark so much over the last few years, but not seeing her get married to Ben would be too much.

It wasn't only her parents, but Ben's mother she had to think about. Her future mother-in-law was due to arrive later that day. The two women had never met before and Meera was feeling a little nervous. Agnes Bannister was a widow who, after visiting Ben's sister in Australia, was stopping in Yorkshire on her way back home to Scotland. Ben had suggested it might be easier for her to stay at the White Hart while they finished decorating, but Meera wouldn't hear of it. Ben had been so welcoming to her family, she wanted to do same for the only relative of his she was likely to meet.

She'd taken the afternoon off work to prepare for Agnes's arrival. She'd made the bed up in the newly painted spare room with fresh linen and placed a vase of pale pink roses on the dressing table. They were the freshest she could find in Thirsk market, and she hoped Agnes would appreciate them. Ben had been fairly vague when she'd asked him what his mother's favourite flowers were. He hadn't been much help when it came to choosing what cake she should make to serve with tea when Agnes arrived either.

"Don't go to too much bother, Meera. She won't like a fuss," was all he kept saying.

In the end, Meera had decided to play it safe and make a lemon drizzle and a Victoria sponge. She checked her watch. It was almost time to collect Krish from school, then she should have almost enough time to help him with his homework before Ben collected his mother from the station.

She parked her car on the cobbles outside the school and thought she'd relax for a few minutes listening to some classical music on the radio. As she leaned back against the headrest she caught sight of Caroline leaving the vicarage in the rear-view mirror. Suddenly, she remembered she had a leaflet in her pocket she wanted to pass on. She was determined to at least get her patient to consider having treatment. She closed the car door and hurried towards the stubborn dowager, but Caroline, who looked even sterner than usual, didn't stop or even slow down.

"I'm sorry, Dr Kumar. I really don't have time to talk today."

Meera watched opened-mouthed as Caroline marched back to the dower house. She really wasn't an easy woman to help. The shrill ringing of the school bell distracted her, and she arrived at the gate as Krish came charging out, proudly waving a ten-out-of-ten maths test. Unfortunately, this triumph, meant a visit to Nora at the village shop for celebratory sweets. It seemed several other parents had the same idea. The place was packed. On the counter was a cardboard box full of fireworks with a handwritten 'half-price sale' notice stuck on the front.

"This is down to you, this is," Nora grumbled pointing to the box as soon as she saw Meera. "You and that campaign of yours has damaged my business."

"I'm sorry to hear that, Mrs Parkin," replied Meera politely, not wanting to get into a discussion with the unpleasant woman.

"I bet it would be a different story if it was one of your festivals."

"One of my festivals?" replied Meera coolly. Although she'd suspected Nora was a bigot, everyone in Hartwell had always treated her with the utmost respect. However, she'd had plenty of experience of this casual racism growing up and she knew the best way of dealing with it was to confront it head-on. The other customers in the shop had all stopped to watch and listen.

"Yes, wasn't it you lot who invented fireworks in the first place?" replied Nora who obviously didn't care if she had an audience or not.

"I think you will find that was the Chinese, but perhaps all us Asians look the same to you, Mrs Parkin."

And with that she took her son's hand and marched out the door, leaving Nora gaping like a goldfish.

"Wow, Mum. You were fierce!" gasped Krish, staring up at her in awe as they stepped outside.

"It's important to speak up for yourself," she replied, then realising this might contradict other instructions she'd given over the years, "but you should always be polite to your elders. I'm sorry you missed out on your sweets. There is cake at home."

"Cool," replied Krish cheerfully.

Despite her best efforts to appear calm, Meera could feel her heart racing as she drove home. She hated confrontation. Then as she turned into the driveway of the Grange, she saw a tall woman with short grey hair standing at her front door with a large suitcase by her feet. She was wearing a long coat, bobble hat and knitted scarf.

"Hello, may I help you?" she asked as she stepped out of her car.

"I am here to see my son. This is the address he gave me," said the woman in a slight Scottish accent and without a hint of a smile. Feeling slightly flustered, Meera stepped forward. Inexplicably, Ben had no photos of his family, but this must surely be his mother.

"Mrs Bannister?" she queried tentatively. "Hello, I'm Meera and this is Krish."

There was an awkward pause. Meera's instinct was to hug the new arrival, but Agnes Bannister didn't even hold out her hand and instead bent down and picked up her suitcase.

"Oh, let me take that for you," offered Meera immediately as she unlocked the front door. "I'm sorry Ben isn't here. There must have been some confusion—he's gone to York to collect you from the station."

"He shouldn't have bothered. I took an early train. London is a horrible, dirty, noisy place. I wanted to leave as soon as possible."

"Hopefully, you'll find Yorkshire more peaceful," said Meera. "Why don't you go through to the drawing room, and I'll make us all some tea. Krish will show you the way."

Meera hurried through into the kitchen and immediately called Ben, but he wasn't picking up, so instead she left a message telling him to come home as his mother was already here.

When she returned to the drawing room with a tea tray laden down with her freshly baked cakes, she found Krish and Agnes sitting in silence.

"Would you like some Victoria sponge or some lemon drizzle cake, or perhaps a slice of each?" offered Meera, only to be met with Agnes pulling a face that made her look like she was sucking lemons.

"No, thank you. I don't care for anything that sweet. Do you perhaps have some fruit loaf or a plain scone?"

"No, I'm sorry," replied Meera, her knife still poised above the cakes. "I think I have some shortbread biscuits in the tin. I didn't make them myself, but they are very nice."

Agnes shook her head. "No, thank you. I'm always disappointed by shop-bought shortbread, particularly if it was made in England. I'm sure you understand."

Meera nodded, but she didn't understand the woman sitting opposite her at all. She busied herself by cutting Krish a large slice of his favourite Victoria sponge.

"Please can I take this upstairs, Mum? I've got loads of homework to do."

"Yes, you go ahead," she replied and watched as her son practically ran out of the room.

THE NEXT HOUR was the longest of Meera's life. She tried time and time again to make conversation with the woman whose son she was due to marry, only to be met with one-word answers. When Ben finally walked through the door, she could have wept with relief. Then she watched in fascination as he walked across the room and rather formally kissed Agnes on the cheek.

"Hello, Mother. It's good to see you."

"Hello, Benedict. Are you well?"

"Good thanks. Sorry I missed you at the station. You should have told me which train you were on—I'd have come for you." He sat down next to Meera, but before he could kiss her hello or she could offer him some cake, Agnes was on her feet.

"Now you are here, will you carry my case up to my room? It is quite a weight. Your girlfriend offered, but she doesn't look very strong."

Meera tried not to bridle at being addressed this way. Agnes had yet to use her name, but she still remained polite.

"That's a good idea. Why don't you settle in. Supper should be ready in about half an hour. It's salmon en croute. I hope you like it."

There was the face again. "It sounds a little heavy. I try not to eat too much before I go to bed. Could I have a bowl of soup in my room? Something out of a tin is fine, if you don't make your own."

Ben and his mother left the room and Meera trudged back to the kitchen and poured a can of tomato soup into a saucepan. She'd been looking forward to showing her guest up to her bedroom, but now she was relieved Ben was doing that instead.

"She hates me," whispered Meera as soon as Ben reappeared.

"Of course, she doesn't," replied Ben. "She's only just met you."

"She hasn't smiled once, and she won't touch anything I've made."

"It's only her way. Everyone laughs at me not having any social graces. Well, now you know where I get it from." He kissed her neck. "Now, let me take that soup up to her and we can enjoy our supper in peace."

Meera lifted the pastry salmon out of the oven as Krish arrived in the kitchen too. They all sat down at the table. Ben and Krish began devouring the salmon Meera had lovingly prepared, but she had no appetite. She considered Ben's explanation. It was true that he could be a little direct, some would say blunt, but he was always friendly. She would have liked to talk things over with Ben some more, but no sooner had he placed his knife and fork together, than his phone bleeped, and he was called out to one of Rachel's many uncles whose prize bull had gone lame.

Meera cleared away the plates, then went to check on Krish who had disappeared back to his room. She made sure he had finished his homework, brushed his teeth and kissed him goodnight. As she closed his door and walked back across the landing, she shivered. She placed a hand on the radiator. The heating was definitely on, so why did the place feel this cold? Tentatively, she knocked on Agnes's bedroom door.

"Yes," called out a muffled voice. Meera opened the door and stepped inside. Agnes was sitting up in bed. She was wearing her coat, hat and scarf. The window was wide open and the curtains were billowing in the wind.

"Hello," said Meera. "Aren't you cold with the window open?"

"Of course, I am. Why do you think I'm dressed like this? But the place smells so strongly of paint it was giving me a headache."

"Would you like to move to a different room?" offered Meera.

"No, no I don't want to be any bother. Do you have a hot water bottle?"

"No, I'm sorry we don't," apologised Meera, suddenly feeling very inadequate. "I have some extra blankets in the airing cupboard."

"No, no. That wouldn't do at all. I would never sleep with all that extra weight pressing down on me. No, I'll have to make the best of it. Goodnight."

And with that, Agnes flicked off the bedside light and turned her back to Meera. It was like a slap in the face.

"Goodnight," replied Meera quietly closing the door behind her. Then she made her way downstairs, slightly numb from both cold and shock.

As she entered the kitchen, she heard a car pull up outside. Thinking it was Ben finally home, she opened the back door with relief, only to find her brother walking towards her.

"Nish! What are you doing here at this hour? Is everything okay? Has something happened to Mum or Dad?"

"Chill, Meera! I'm just dropping off a new Xbox headset for Krish," replied her younger brother testily as he walked past her and into the kitchen. "Can I go and give it to him?"

"No, he's gone to bed and doesn't he already have a headset?"

"This is the latest version. It was only released yesterday.

They're really hard to get hold of. A mate managed to get me one."

"Oh well thank you. That was kind," replied Meera, although she was always slightly dubious about some of the business practices of Nish's many mates. "You didn't come all the way out here to drop it off, did you?"

"No, I'm on my way to pick up Becky. She finishes her shift at the pub at half ten."

"Isn't it a little late to be going on a date?" queried Meera, who would normally have been tucked up in bed by now if she wasn't feeling so agitated.

"Don't be such an old granny! We're going to a club in Harrogate—nobody will even show up before midnight."

"Oh my goodness! How does Becky ever get up in the morning to take Minty to school?"

"Give it a rest, Meera. Seriously, you're starting to sound like Mum."

"I'm happy for you, but I am a little surprised the two of you are spending so much time together. I wouldn't have thought you have much in common."

"Really? She grew up with an older sister, who always did better at school than her, who her parents always turned to first for help and advice. Sound familiar?"

Meera held up her hands. "Okay, okay, there's no need to be so angry. I was only trying to offer some advice." Meera paused, trying to pick her words carefully. "After all, her situation is a little complicated."

Nish narrowed his eyes and shook his head. "Becky's life is complicated? Take a look at your own situation. You really can be a hypocrite sometimes, Meera."

Then he turned and stomped out. As she heard him slam the back door behind him, Meera slumped down into the nearest chair and gave a deep sigh. A second later Darwin scurried into the room and jumped up on her lap. For once she didn't mind that Krish had forgotten to lock him in his cage for the night. Instead, she gave him a small smile and tickled his ears affectionately. "At least you look pleased to see me. I seem to have upset everyone else today."

CHAPTER SEVEN

J O WASN'T HAVING a good night either. Outside the wind
was rattling the window frame as heavy raindrops pelted
the glass. Inside the only light was coming from the screen of
her phone. It cast a pale, eerie glow across the room. Next to
her Jack snored loudly, but she couldn't sleep. Instead, she
was silently terrifying herself. She had begun googling cures
for morning sickness. Despite the amount of abuse she'd
given her body, it had never let her down before. She hadn't
taken a day off sick in her life, and she hated not knowing
when this nausea would end.

The googling had led to options on how to give birth
and now she was on to possible birth defects. All the things
that could wrong. Genetically this and that. She'd never
known her parents or any of her family. What problems
might there be that she didn't know about? All she did know
was that the only thing her mother had thought to leave her
with was a necklace that linked her to Hartwell. Jack was
adamant that this meant her mother or father must have
been from the village. A terrible thought suddenly struck her.
It made her feel sicker than she had all day.

"Jack!" she whispered urgently. "Jack!"

There was no response so she delivered a quick kick to

his shin. He stopped snoring.

"Wake up," she hissed, reaching over and shaking his shoulder.

"What is it? What's wrong? Have you been sick again?" he murmured, his eyes still closed.

Jo gave him another shake. "Could Shirley be my mother?"

Jack's eyes pinged open. "What?"

"Is it possible Shirley could be my mother?"

Jack slowly sat up and rested on his elbow. "No of course she isn't. Why would you think such a thing?" Then spotting the phone lying on the duvet, he picked it up and squinted at the screen. "Oh, Jo, you shouldn't be reading this stuff. You'll scare yourself to death."

"I need to be prepared. Meera said so."

"She meant getting plenty of rest and giving up the cigs. You'll never get any sleep if you fill your head with all of this."

"But there are so many things that can go wrong. They keep saying it could be to do with genetics or something they inherit, but I don't know anything about my genes and don't make a joke about me always wearing Levi's."

"I wasn't going to."

"What if we are related? Closely related. That could be terrible. The baby could have all sorts of problems."

"Jo, seriously, you're overreacting. I think Mum might have mentioned if we were related by now."

"Maybe she doesn't know. Didn't you say she went for auditions in London when she wanted to be an actress? She could have had me when she was down there."

"That was before she got married and had me. Years before you were born." He placed a hand gently on her shoulder. "Seriously, Jo, I'm no doctor, but this stress can't be good for you or the baby."

Jo flopped back on her pillow. She knew he was right.

"Whatever," she sighed, "but I think it's time I finally took your advice. I need to find out about my past."

"Good, but can we at least wait until it's light?"

THE NEXT MORNING, she was sitting at her desk, alone in the office. Since announcing her pregnancy she'd been flooded with congratulations from officers she hadn't even spoken to before. She'd also been put on lighter duties. The rest of CID had gone to investigate a gang of poachers who they believed were living in a caravan up on the moors. She hadn't gone with them. The thought of a long, bumpy drive over narrow farm tracks without any loos nearby sounded like hell right now.

Dawson had left her a report to read about a spate of farm vehicle thefts that had taken place when she was away in London. She'd flicked through it for a few seconds before pushing it to one side. Then she reached for a pad of paper and a pen and quickly started to write down the names of all the women in Hartwell she could think of who could be old enough to be her mother.

Shirley, Joan, Mary, Caroline. Then with a shudder she added Nora's name.

"Please don't let it be her," she said under her breath.

Next, she added all the names of Rachel's aunts she could remember, then paused and stared at the list. There were a dozen names, but it was quite possible that none of them was the right one. If her mother had ever lived in Hartwell she could have moved away long ago. Surely, if she was still in the village, she would have realised who Jo was and said something?

She shook her head impatiently. She wasn't thinking clearly. She needed to distance herself, treat this like it was an investigation. To have given her baby away, her mother must have been desperate. What was the reason? Was she young and unmarried? That could apply to at least three of the aunts, but the Foxtons were such a close family she could only imagine them all rallying around if one of them was in trouble. Sending one of their clan down to London to have a baby and making her give it away seemed highly unlikely.

Perhaps her mother was married, but her husband wasn't the father. She knew Caroline, Joan, Shirley and Mary would all have been married when she was born. Three of them were widowed now, so there would be no reason to keep quiet still. At that moment, her phone pinged. It was a text from Jack.

Checked with Mum. We are def NOT related but she now thinks I've totally lost the plot.

Jo smiled to herself as she drew a line through Shirley's name. There was another text.

Don't worry. We'll find out who your parents are. Promise xx

Jo sighed. She knew Jack would do anything he could to help her, but she also knew the people of Hartwell could be very good at keeping secrets. She was about to text him back when she heard the sound of heavy footsteps coming down the corridor. She quickly tore the page out, folded it and slipped it into her pocket as the chief constable appeared in the doorway.

"Sergeant Ormond. Good to see you back. Feeling better, I hope?" he asked.

Jo quickly got to her feet. "Yes. Thank you, sir."

"Sit down, sit down. We have been contacted by the Met and Inspector Wallace personally asked for your assistance."

"What with, sir?" asked Jo. She could feel her heart racing. Wallace was her old boss. Ironically, it was when she was off on maternity leave that Jo had been sent up to Yorkshire, after an operation had gone wrong under the direction of Inspector Palmer, who was covering for Wallace and had taken an instant dislike to Jo. If Wallace was back, maybe there was a chance she'd get back to London after all, but she couldn't let herself get carried away. The chief constable was talking again, and she needed to concentrate.

"It seems her team are investigating a possible connection between two suspected armed robbers and the death of Lord Hanley," he explained. "The guns they used were registered to him."

Jo nodded. She already knew all this thanks to a visit from Simon Spencer, one of her ex-colleagues.

"But Lord Hanley wasn't shot, sir."

"No but, as I'm sure you remember, there was a slight fracture to the skull. The pathology report couldn't determine whether it killed him. The officers in London are working on the theory that he may have been hit with the butt of the gun. I get the impression they want another charge to bring against them in case they don't secure a conviction with the first. Between you and me, I think it sounds a little far-fetched. However, if there is enough evidence, we could reopen the investigation into Hanley's death and work alongside Wallace and her team."

Jo felt a rush of excitement. An official joint investigation with Scotland Yard. Was Rupert's death going to be her way back to London after all?

"What do you want me to do, sir?" she asked, trying to sound calm.

"It could take a while, but seeing as you are desk-bound for the time being, I didn't think you'd mind. The two suspects are saying they bought the guns from an auction. Unfortunately, they can't recall which one, nor do they have any paperwork to support this claim. I recall you visited Hartwell Hall and discovered the guns were missing, so you have all the details. I want you to contact all the auction houses that specialise in firearms sales and see if there is any truth in what the two suspects are saying."

"I'll get on it straight away, sir," she replied eagerly.

Four hours and far too many cups of weak, milky tea later, Jo was finally making progress. She had found an online catalogue for a small but prestigious specialist firearms auctioneer in Marylebone. There were no pictures, but the description sounded like Rupert's guns, though she needed to be sure. After a little more digging she discovered that the same auction house had been robbed before the sale the guns were listed in. She phoned the director of the company, but so far he was proving to be less than helpful.

"You must understand, our customers expect the highest level of discretion, Sergeant Ormond."

Jo raised her eyes to the ceiling.

"All I need is their name," she insisted.

"Perhaps I could contact the seller and request their permission to speak to you."

"There isn't time. Can I remind you this is a criminal investigation? I just need a name."

There was a long pause.

"Lady Hanley asked us to sell the guns."

Jo froze her pen in mid-air above the notebook. This was the last thing she'd expected. She'd been working on the assumption Rupert had tried selling the guns to raise some cash to feed his habit.

"Thanks," she mumbled, but the silence at the other end of the line told her he had already gone. She dropped her pen on to the notepad and leaned back in her chair. Her mind went back to the day she'd first visited Lucy at Hartwell Hall. She had been sent to the village to check all the licensed guns in the village. Lucy had opened the gun cabinet to find it was empty. She'd seemed completely shocked. Was it possible she'd been lying all along? If she'd sold the guns, couldn't she have told Jo that?

Then another thought hit her. Lucy wasn't the only Lady Hanley in Hartwell. Grabbing her coat and car keys, Jo headed for the door. If she was going to speak to Caroline, she wanted to do it face to face. In her experience, it was rare for the older Lady Hanley to show any emotion, but she wanted to be there to catch any slight reaction she might have when Jo asked her about the guns.

It was growing dark when she pulled up outside the dower house. The outside lantern above the front door cast a golden glow over the gravel path. She was about to push open the wrought-iron gate when she saw Shirley step out of the door and come towards her. She stopped with a start when she saw Jo.

"Hello, love, what are you doing here?"

"I need to speak to Caroline about something. Is she in?"

"Yes, we've been having a bit of a natter." She came forward and gave Jo a hug before stepping back and looking at her. "How was work today?"

Jo shrugged. "Okay, I guess."

"Well don't overdo it. You still look a little pale."

As Shirley crunched away down the path, Jo approached the front door and, after lifting the brass knocker shaped like a lion's head, knocked loudly twice. A few seconds later, it was opened by Caroline. She looked surprised and at first she didn't say anything—she simply stared at Jo.

"Hello," said Jo, "I'm sorry to disturb you."

"I thought you were Shirley coming back," said Caroline, regaining her composure.

"Yes, I've just seen her. Can I come in?"

Caroline moved to one side and Jo stepped into the hall. Caroline led her through into the drawing room. Jo had only been here once before when she was checking the gun that Caroline owned. Oil paintings in gilt frames covered the walls and the place was crammed full of well-polished antique furniture. A Siamese cat was stretched out asleep on the rug, in front of a roaring fire.

"Please take a seat," said Caroline, gesturing to the sofa as she sat down in the armchair opposite. Jo perched on the edge of the cushion. The place felt like a museum—one wrong move and she was sure to break something. She decided to dive straight in.

"I want to ask you about a pair of guns that belonged to your son."

"Guns?" Caroline stared at Jo. If she'd had to describe the look on her face, Jo would have said she looked relieved more than anything.

"Yes. When I first arrived here, Lucy told me they were missing. We believe they were given to an auction house to be sold. When I spoke to someone at the auction house, they told me they received instructions from Lady Hanley, but they didn't say if it was you or Lucy."

"It was me," Caroline said briskly, suddenly looking and sounding more like her usual self.

"May I ask why?"

"As I am sure you are aware, Rupert had become addicted to drugs. When under their influence, he had a tendency to become violent. I thought it better for all concerned if the shotguns were removed from Hartwell Hall."

"You thought he might shoot Lucy? Had he ever threatened her? Did she ask you to take them?"

"No, she did not. I'm not sure if he ever threatened her with them directly. Lucy tends to see the best in people. I doubt she would have taken him seriously. She spent a long time making excuses for him and his behaviour."

"Why didn't you tell her you'd removed the guns?"

"I didn't want to worry her."

"But surely…" Jo began, but Caroline interrupted her.

"How do you suggest I should have broached the subject, Sergeant Ormond? I am taking your husband's guns so he can't shoot you, Lucinda? To be quite honest, I didn't expect her to notice they were missing. You know how vague she can be. And I was right—she didn't notice until you paid her a visit."

Jo thought back to that day. "I came here after I'd been to Hartwell Hall. I asked you about the missing guns. Why didn't you tell me you'd taken them?"

"I am not in the habit of telling strangers my business."

Jo didn't waste her breath warning Caroline that she had been withholding evidence.

"Why sell them? Why not keep them here?" she asked instead.

Caroline glanced down at her hands and adjusted her gold wedding band.

"That was my idea initially, but when Rupert disappeared, it seemed more sensible to sell them. They were quite valuable, and I thought the money they would raise could be put to better use maintaining the hall."

"You didn't think Rupert would come back? Get over his addiction, and maybe want them back?"

Caroline fixed her pale blue eyes on Jo. "No, I did not," she replied without further elaboration.

Jo tried a different tack. She had the feeling Caroline was holding something back, but she didn't know what. "Don't you lot usually hold on to stuff like guns? Pass them on to father and son."

Caroline arched an eyebrow and her lips twitched into something close to a smile. "You lot? My goodness, you make me sound quite alien, but yes, it is true that had Rupert lived, I'm sure Freddie would have inherited the guns at some point; however, my grandson has shown absolutely no interest in shooting and his mother has positively discouraged it."

"Don't you approve?"

"Actually, I do. Allowing the Hanley tradition of males killing things to die out is one of the few things Lucinda and I agree on." Her face softened a little. "Freddie adores animals. If he ever takes aim at the local wildlife, I feel sure it will only be with a camera."

Not for the first time, Jo was struck by the thought that Caroline only really sounded human when she was talking about her grandson.

"I assume you know the auction house was broken into?" she asked.

"Yes, I was informed. I have to say, I would have hoped a place in central London crammed full of valuable weapons would have had better security arrangements in place, but at least our guns were covered by their insurance so the estate will be reimbursed, although they do seem to be dragging their feet rather."

"Did you go down to London to take them to the auction house?"

"I did."

"Do you visit London often?"

"I go occasionally, to the theatre, to visit friends, or my doctor."

"You go to a London doctor, not Meera or Dr Robertson when he was here."

"Dr Kumar seems extremely competent, but unfortunately the same could not be said of her predecessor. Forgive me, Sergeant Ormond, but what has my choice of medical professional to do with stolen guns?"

Jo felt herself flush. "I was only trying to make conversation," she mumbled, then clearing her throat: "the thing is. Your guns, the ones that were stolen, were used in an armed robbery. My colleagues in London arrested the two men involved. They were already known to the police in connection with drug offences rather than robbery." She paused. "And we know they supplied drugs to your son."

Caroline's blank expression had returned. "What a strange coincidence."

"We're investigating if it could be more than a coincidence. Whether the two men involved in the robbery could also have been responsible for Rupert's death."

"I understood the investigation into my son's death was closed."

"Don't you want to know what happened to him? If anyone else was involved, don't you want to see them brought to justice? To be punished?"

Caroline rose to her feet. "Would it bring my son back to me? No, it would not. We've all been through enough as far as Rupert is concerned. I would prefer to let sleeping dogs lie."

Jo stood up too and began to make her way back into the hall. "I'm afraid it's not your decision or mine. If the team in London think they could secure a murder conviction as well as armed robbery, they'll want to pursue the case."

"No doubt you will keep me informed, Sergeant Ormond," replied Caroline as she opened the front door. "Before you go, I understand congratulations are in order."

"Thanks," mumbled Jo, rather awkwardly, before stepping out on to the path. She exhaled loudly as she climbed into her car. It looked like her day had been wasted. She'd like to bet the two guys arrested down in London were involved with the robbery at the auction house, but she was no closer to linking them to Rupert's death or to getting back to London herself. More to the point, she had recently started questioning whether that was what she still wanted. Could she really make Jack leave Hartwell? Raising a child here with all the fresh air and space, and with Shirley and her friends so eager to help, would be much easier than the two of them struggling alone in London.

But could she resign herself to the fact that she would never again get that buzz from working on the sort of big case only the Met could offer her?

IT TOOK LESS than a minute to drive home. The cottage was in darkness when she pulled up on to the cobbles outside. There was a note on the kitchen table from Jack saying he'd had to go into work because Becky had called in sick. Jo leaned wearily against the table. Her own stomach was beginning to churn again too. She really should follow Meera's advice. She kept telling her to eat a little and often, but she hadn't had anything since ten o'clock that morning when Dawson had brought her a bacon sandwich from the canteen. Perhaps she should have some of Joan's magic ginger tea. Jack normally made it for her, but how hard could it be?

The recipe was taped to the front of the cupboard above the kettle. Jo scanned the ingredients: *Ginger, honey, nutmeg...* Then she paused. At the bottom of the recipe, Joan had written: *I hope you feel better soon, love Joan.* There was something about the writing that looked familiar. She left the kettle boiling and hurried upstairs. In her bedroom she yanked open the drawer of the bedside cabinet and rummaged through until she found it. There it was nestled beneath her passport, the note she'd been left with outside the hospital. It was written on thick, good quality card and was about the same size as a postcard. It simply read: *Her name is Jo. Please take good care of her. Thank you.* The card was dog-eared and marked with greasy fingerprints.

Jo had been given the note along with the Hartwell noble she wore around her neck by her social worker when she turned eighteen. She had spent hours poring over that note, hoping it might hold some hidden meaning, some clue to her parents or her past. Finally, in frustration, she'd given up and stored it away with all the other papers she barely looked at.

Taking it back downstairs she compared it to the recipe. She was sure they had been written by the same person. The capital J for both Jo and Joan had the same distinctive slant and the y's were written with the same unusual loop. Her mind raced. What did she know about Joan? Lucy's kindly housekeeper was an amazing cook and had lived in the gatehouse with her husband for thirty-odd years. She clucked around Lucy and Freddie like a mother hen, but as far as she knew, Joan and Bill had no children of their own. She was sure Lucy had mentioned she'd been a nurse when she was younger. Might she have worked down in London?

She looked down at the note again. Jo, the same first two letters of Joan's name. Over the years, she'd wondered why whoever had left the note had been so insistent about what she should be called. Was this the reason?

Suddenly, she felt quite exhausted. She sank down on to one of the chairs and rested her head on the table. If this had been a work investigation, she would be making phone calls, searching the internet, even driving up to the gatehouse. But this wasn't work, this was her life and for the first time she felt like she might be close to finding out the truth and she was scared. Very, very scared.

CHAPTER EIGHT

IT WAS SLOWLY growing light as Rachel left her cottage and jogged across the cobbles. Her warm breath formed little clouds in front of her as the pale sun tried to break through the early morning mist. As she turned the corner, she spotted Jo leaning against her car and half-heartedly stretching her quads. Rachel ran down to join her. The only other person she'd seen so far this morning was her uncle Frank who delivered milk to the village.

She'd started joining Jo and Jack on their early morning runs about a month ago. Since Sarah had moved in with her, she'd been happy and content. Unfortunately, as far as Rachel was concerned, content equalled chubby. Going out for dinner together or cooking elaborate meals at home while sharing a bottle of wine, had soon seen her piling on the pounds. Annoyingly, Sarah was like Lucy and never put on an ounce no matter how much she ate, but Rachel had to work to stay in shape.

"Isn't Jack joining us?" she asked as Jo jogged up to meet her. She had abandoned her usual shorts and vest for leggings and an oversized hoodie.

"No. He's walking the colonel's dogs, then he said he had to wait for a delivery from the brewery, but I think he was pleased to have an excuse to get away from me for a bit."

"Don't be daft—he's crazy about you and he's over the moon about becoming a dad."

"He is, but I think I've been driving him mad going on about trying to find out who my parents might have been."

Rachel looked at her in surprise. "Ahh, so you've finally decided to look into your past."

"I thought it was time." She paused and glanced over to Rachel. "You're related to almost everyone around here. Has anyone ever mentioned an unwanted pregnancy, maybe a girl getting pregnant when she wasn't married?"

Rachel frowned and shook her head. "No, I don't think so. I'm sorry. I remember mentioning your story to Mum and telling her you had a noble. I'm sure she would have said something if she knew about your background."

"That's what Jack said about Shirley. I just find it weird that nobody knows anything. My parents must have had some connection to Hartwell, otherwise why leave me the noble?"

"I can always ask Mum again," she offered. She couldn't comprehend what it must be like not to know anything about your family. Even if her aunts sometimes drove her mad with their gossiping and interfering, she loved being part of a huge clan and was proud that she had been able to trace her ancestors back for centuries.

"Would you? I haven't really got a lot to go on except this necklace," she said, self-consciously touching the ancient coin that hung around her neck. A passing car beeped at them as it drove by. They both turned to wave. It was Joan. Her little hatchback was proudly displaying a 'Vote Hanley' sticker in the purple and green colours Lucy had chosen.

"Looks like Lucy is serious," commented Rachel with a wry smile, but Jo seemed distracted. "You okay?" she asked.

"I was just thinking, it's good she's got Joan and Bill, as well as Rob for support," replied Jo.

"Yes, those two would do anything for her."

"They don't have any children of their own though, do they?"

"No, I don't think they could. It's a real shame. They both love children. Joan even used to be a paediatric nurse."

"Was that when she was down in London?"

"Yes, then she came back up here to marry Bill. They were childhood sweethearts like Mum and Dad. The four of them used to double date. Before his accident, Dad and Bill would always sneak off for a pint while Mum and Joan were cooking Sunday lunch."

By this time, they had arrived in the churchyard.

"It's no good. I can't go any farther," gasped Jo, as she came to a halt. "I haven't got any energy. I bet even Dawson could outrun me now. Maybe I should switch to cycling. Shirley has an old bike I could use."

She flopped down on to the wooden bench as Rachel continued to jog on the spot.

"Take your time. You shouldn't push yourself," she said as she felt a pang of guilt. "And I'm sorry about going on about my parents, when you are trying to find yours."

"Don't be stupid. It's great you've got happy memories, especially now your dad isn't around anymore."

Rachel's eyes automatically drifted over to where her father was buried. "It would have been his sixty-eighth birthday today," she said quietly. "I'm going to take Mum into Thirsk and get some flowers later."

"You must both really miss him. I guess at least I've been spared that."

The two of them were silent for a moment, lost in their thoughts, then Rachel nodded towards the church. "Have you thought about looking in the parish records or speaking to Reverend Davenport?"

"Not really why?"

"He's been here for over thirty years. People in desperate situations might turn to the church for help. Mum said his memory is going a bit, but maybe he remembers someone coming to him for advice or something."

Jo nodded thoughtfully. "You could be right. Thanks, Rachel, I appreciate it."

Rachel shrugged as she joined Jo on the bench. "No problem." Then she glanced down at her feet. "Actually I was going to ask you for a favour too."

"Go ahead," said Jo sounding a little surprised.

"If Sarah asks, can you tell her that I came back to your cottage for an hour after our run?"

Jo raised an eyebrow. "Sure, any particular reason why?"

"Lucy texted me last night to ask me to go up to the Hall for a chat and Sarah can be a bit funny about me seeing her. Sometimes it's easier not to mention it."

Rachel fiddled with the end of her plait self-consciously. When Sarah had moved in, she had promised there would be no secrets between them, but sharing her life with someone after living alone for so long was proving to be more difficult than she'd imagined.

Jo, however, didn't pass any judgement she just closed her eyes and leaned back. "Fair enough. Why don't you jog up to the Hall now. I'm knackered anyway—I haven't been sleeping very well. As soon as I get enough energy, I'm going to go home, soak in the bath, then maybe eat a whole tub of chocolate ice cream."

Rachel stood up and grinned. "Have you cleared that with Meera?"

Jo made a face as she pulled up her hood. "No and if I'm keeping your secrets, you can do the same for me. I've given up cigs, booze and coffee. I've got to have some vices."

Rachel left Jo basking in the early morning sun and jogged off in the direction of Hartwell Hall. Along the way, she passed two huge hoardings that had been placed in fields belonging to the estate. They were emblazoned with 'Vote Hanley' and had a photo of a smiling Lucy, dressed casually and holding a baby lamb. It was actually Rachel who had taken the photo earlier in the year when Lucy had brought Freddie and Krish up to the farm to see the lambs. The image was certainly different from the photos the candidates from the three main parties were using, with their sombre suits and serious expressions. Only Heather Rhodes looked human, if a little earnest in her poster, as she stood on a windswept moor wearing her anorak and hiking boots.

"I see you are serious about standing in the by-election?" she said as the entered the kitchen at Hartwell Hall and found Freddie and Lucy busily folding campaign leaflets.

"Absolutely. I'll be amazed if anyone actually votes for me, but it's the best way I can think of drawing attention to the lack of funding for the Rosemary Centre. If I cause enough noise, maybe one of the other candidates will realise how important an issue it is and campaign for it to be funded properly too."

"Any luck so far?"

"Alison said Heather, your old teacher, has offered to volunteer at the centre, but nothing from the other candidates. Alison did say they've seen an increase in donations since I announced I was standing though, so that's something too."

"I'll take over here if you want to escape, Freddie," Rachel offered.

Freddie turned to Lucy. "Is that okay, Mum?" he asked hopefully.

"Yes, of course. Thanks for your help!" she called after him, as he and the dogs scurried out of the back door.

Rachel took his seat and started folding. "These look good. Really professional."

"Thanks. Nish got them printed for me. Apparently, he has a mate in the trade."

"So, what did you want to talk to me about?"

"I wanted to ask you a favour. I need a campaign manager. Is there any chance you'd be able to do it? You'd be brilliant."

Rachel stopped folding, looked down at her hands and was silent for a moment before replying. "I'd love to help you, Lucy, I really would, but I'm not sure it's such a good idea. Things are going really well with Sarah, and I would hate to do anything to rock the boat. She knows how I used to feel about you and…"

Lucy flushed a deep shade of red. "Yes, of course, I completely understand. It was thoughtless of me to ask. Forget I said anything."

Rachel reached across and gave her hand a squeeze. "For what it's worth, you definitely have my vote."

Lucy gave her a small smile. "Thanks." She counted on her fingers. "With you, Rob, Jack, Jo, Meera, Ben, Joan, Bill and Shirley, I might actually reach double figures."

"You'll get a lot more than that. I'll marshal all the Foxtons and that way you'll hit a hundred easily," replied Rachel with a grin. She started folding again, while Lucy stood up and filled the kettle at the sink.

"This is going to bring you loads of publicity. Are you ready for that? The press and maybe your opponents are going to start digging about in your personal life, especially with Guy's trial due to start soon. They'll probably drag up everything about Rupert too."

Lucy nodded. "I know, but thanks to Mum's book, everything is going to come out anyway. At least now I get to put my side of the story over. Freddie knows how things were between Rupert and me, so it won't come as a shock to him. I've warned him that people might gossip about me. Bless him, he said he didn't care and that he thinks I'll make a great politician."

"You'd certainly be an improvement on our last one." Lucy shuddered at Rachel's reference to Guy. "It seems pretty unfair that you all have to go to court and give evidence when, he doesn't."

Lucy brought two mugs of tea over to the table. "They say it's because he's too ill. Speaking of trials, isn't Max due to court any day now?"

"Yes, it was yesterday."

"Did you go?"

"No. He's pleading guilty so I didn't need to and I had absolutely no desire to see him again. I don't think Mum and Becky went either."

"It's been a crazy year." Lucy sighed.

Rachel took a sip of tea and gestured towards the pile of leaflets. "It has and by the look of things, it's only going to get crazier."

WHEN RACHEL FINALLY left Hartwell Hall, the morning's sun had disappeared behind heavy, grey clouds. Rather than going straight home, she jogged back through the drizzle and puddles to her mother's farmhouse. Since they'd lost her dad all anniversaries and birthdays were difficult—she wanted to make sure her mother wasn't feeling too low. She found Mary in the kitchen, humming quietly along to the radio as she rolled out some pastry.

"Hello, love. This is a nice surprise," she said brushing the flour from her hands as Rachel came through the door.

"I wanted to make sure you were okay, today. To let you know I was thinking of you," Rachel said as she hugged her mother.

"It's good of you to remember," said Mary her eyes beginning to fill with tears.

"How could I ever forget?" replied Rachel softly.

"I know it's silly, but I thought I'd make an apple pie. It was his favourite."

"You finish what you were doing. I'll make us both a cup of tea."

Mary dabbed at her eyes with the bottom of her apron, before picking up her rolling pin again, while Rachel went to fill the kettle, pausing briefly to fuss Jenny, the old sheepdog.

"Have you heard how it went in court yesterday?" she asked.

"I spoke to the police liaison officer. They said the judge adjourned the case, but that he would be sentenced next week. He warned Max that he would be facing a custodial sentence, but the nice police lady said as he is pleading guilty, it probably won't be more than two years and that he could be out again in less than one."

"How did Becky take the news?"

"I think even though she'd been told what to expect it was still a shock. It didn't help that her divorce papers arrived yesterday too. I suppose it must all feel very final to her."

"Should I go and say something sympathetic to her?" asked Rachel as she carried two mugs of tea over to the table where her mother was now arranging slices of apple on to the base of the pie.

"I don't think she wants to talk about it. Besides, she isn't here. Nish has taken her and Minty to the cinema to see the new Disney film."

Rachel rolled her eyes. So much for Becky being in shock—and why had she left their mum on her own? Had she forgotten what day it was?

"Now, don't look like that," chided Mary. "It's good that she's keeping busy, taking her mind off things, and Nish seems like a very nice young man. Don't you approve?"

Rachel shrugged. "I think she should take things more slowly, but Nish seems okay. He is Meera's brother after all and apparently he's helping Lucy with her campaign to become our MP."

Mary looked up in surprise. "What? Lucy an MP? Becky said something about that. I thought she was joking."

Rachel grinned. Her mother's reaction was typical of everyone else in the village when they heard about Lucy's plan. "I know it's completely mad, but she thought the other candidates were useless, so she put herself forward." She paused. "Part of me wonders if she just wanted a distraction from Sadie's biography and the court case against Guy."

"Poor Lucy." Mary sighed, shaking her head. "She's been through such a lot."

"Let's talk about something more cheerful. Have you heard Jo and Jack are expecting a baby?"

Mary's face immediately brightened. She loved children. "Yes! Isn't it exciting? I don't think Shirley has stopped smiling."

"It's made Jo want to find out about her own parents and if there's really a connection between them and Hartwell. I promised her I would ask you about it again. Was there any gossip or scandal back then?"

Mary turned away and went over to the sink to wash her hands. "My goodness, I can barely remember what happened yesterday, let alone thirty-odd years ago."

"It was probably around thirty-one years ago. Jo turned thirty a few months ago. Me, Jack and Rupert would all have been toddlers," she persisted. "Were there any rumours of an affair or did someone disappear suddenly?"

Mary shook her head. "Nothing springs to mind, love."

Although Mary looked and sounded perfectly normal, Rachel got the distinct impression her mother was hiding something, but before she could press her any further, she changed the subject.

"Actually, I'm pleased you called around. I've been giving a lot of thought to this idea of yours for a heritage centre in the village."

"Really? I thought you were only humouring Sarah."

Rachel and Sarah had gone to the farmhouse for lunch with Mary the previous Sunday and Sarah had explained all their plans in great detail.

"Don't be silly. She had some very interesting ideas, and it sounds exactly the sort of thing the village and you need."

"I need?"

"Yes. You've always been a bit restless. I know you enjoy your job, but you need more of a challenge, something to get your teeth into. So, I was thinking why not use the stables and the old barn. They could easily be converted, and I don't think it would cost anything like as much as Rob would want for the Hayloft."

"Bailey is happy up at Dan's so the stables are empty, but where would you put the tractors if we used the barn?"

"I've been thinking we might not need them much longer. I'm thinking of asking Dan to take on the flock."

"You want to stop farming? But the Foxtons have always farmed here," protested Rachel. She could feel a sense of growing excitement inside her at the thought that their dreams could soon be a reality, but it felt somehow wrong to be talking about this on her dad's birthday.

"Dan's a Foxton. Look, love, I'm not getting any younger." Rachel opened her mouth to protest, but Mary held up her hand. She looked unusually determined. "Max might have been behind all the problems I thought I had, but it did make me realise I shouldn't take my health for granted, and it's sensible to make plans for the future. You know as well as I do that it's getting harder and harder to make money out of farming. Mick and Tony have both talked about wanting to retire in the next few months. I know you've always helped me out with the business side of the farm, but neither you nor your sister want to be sheep farmers. You and Sarah have these plans for creating something new and exciting here in Hartwell and we have a whole range of farm buildings standing empty on the other side of the yard. Why not use them for this scheme you and Sarah have come up with?"

"I don't know what to say," replied Rachel feeling quite overwhelmed.

"You don't have to say anything yet. Why not go and tell Sarah and see what she thinks to the idea?"

RACHEL WAS SO excited to tell Sarah her news, she almost ran back to the cottage. When she arrived, slightly out of breath, she found her in the kitchen peeling carrots. Sarah looked round when she heard the door.

"There you are! Have you been running all this time? You've been gone ages. I'm making a start on lunch," she said.

"I went to see Mum too," replied Rachel.

"Is she okay?"

"Fine and I've found a place for the heritage centre—or rather Mum has."

Sarah put down her knife and turned around in surprise. "In Hartwell?"

"Yes."

"Can we afford it?"

"It won't cost us a thing. At least not in the first instance. We'll still need to renovate it obviously."

"Well, where is it?" demanded Sarah.

Rachel grinned and held out her hand. "Come with me and I'll show you."

Less than five minutes later, they stood outside Bailey's old stable.

"It could be perfect. The first stable could be a ticket office, the second a gift shop, the barn next door is much bigger and has a mezzanine floor so that could house the main exhibition, then the tractor shelter here at the end could be the café. I know it's a bit open to the elements right now, but if we glazed over the entrance the visitors would have a wonderful view of the village. You can actually see the Hayloft from here." Rachel smiled as Sarah gabbled away excitedly. "We could give them a map of the village with their ticket. When they've finished here they could walk down to the burial site and visit the well. How much would it cost?"

"A lot less than buying the Hayloft and hopefully some of the heritage grants you applied for will help. We'll need planning permission for changing the use of the buildings, so we'll need to get the parish council on side and hope nobody else has any objections."

Sarah pushed her red curls away from her face and took Rachel's arm. "Are you sure this is all okay with your mum?"

"She said she wants to wind down the farm and thinks this will be a better use for the buildings."

"Isn't it wonderful that she has such faith in us?"

"It is. Now let's see if we can convince the rest of the village."

CHAPTER NINE

L UCY CURLED UP on the sofa in the library and cringed as she watched a video of herself. When Nish had dropped off the leaflets, he had encouraged her to start using social media in her campaign too and according to him, a few Facebook posts simply wouldn't cut it.

"You need to get the younger voters on side, Luce. The oldies will vote the way they always have," he insisted as he pointed the camera on his phone in her face.

Happily, she was distracted from analysing her performance when Rob returned from his early morning trip to check on the progress of one of his sites in York. He joined her on the sofa and peered at the screen.

"Wow. You're getting a lot of views."

"I can't think why. Does my voice really sound like that?" She sighed as she folded the screen down. "I suppose I shall have to get used to it. I'm being interviewed on local radio later today."

"Well, whatever you are doing it seems to be working. The *Yorkshire Post* has done an opinion poll. You are only a few points behind Devizes."

Lucy picked up the paper and looked at the front page in astonishment. "Really? That can't be right."

"Why not? I'd vote for you; in fact I've asked an agent down in London to try to find a place near Westminster, so we've got somewhere to stay if you need to be down there to vote or debate or whatever."

"Are you serious? Somewhere in central London will cost a fortune. It'll be a total waste of money. I'm not going to win."

"I think you might, and you'll need a base. Besides, I'll want to invest in somewhere else when I eventually sell the Hayloft. If Sarah and her lot ever stop digging up Druids, that is."

"It was very nice of you to let her take all this time."

"She's got big plans for Hartwell. She wants to open some sort of centre about the history of the village. It could be good for the place. Besides, if I hadn't let her, I would have had Rachel to answer to."

Lucy smiled, but Rob wasn't going to be put off.

"So, what do you think to getting a place in London? I was thinking a two-bed apartment, so Freddie has his own room. During term time I'll be up here with him and keeping an eye on everything and you won't need to be down there in the holidays, but there will still be half-terms. If we are all away, Joan and Bill will be able to look after the dogs, so we probably won't need any outside space."

"I'm not sure. Even somewhere small will be terribly expensive and I really don't think I'll win."

"Either way, it could still be a good investment."

Lucy chewed her lip. In truth, she really hadn't considered for one moment she might win this election. Now this opinion poll and Rob's talk of a place in London and being away from Freddie and the dogs sent a wave of panic through her. What had she got herself into? Next to her, Rob shifted his position, so he could look at her directly.

"Is the expense the only reason you are worried about me buying a place in London for us?"

"What do you mean?"

"Are you having doubts about us?"

Lucy stared at him in horror. "No! Why would, I? Are you? Is it the politics thing? I know it's not what you signed up for, but I only really…"

"Hear me out. At the risk of sounding like Jo again, politics is a dirty business. Your opponents will want to get at you and living with a man who has been to prison…" he paused "…they'll use it against you. Now, I don't mind. They can say or write what they want about me, but I saw how upset you were when you saw that article your mum gave the press."

Lucy looked away. The latest instalment of Sadie's biography had been all about how she had hurried back from South Africa to console her only daughter after the mysterious disappearance of her husband. It had gone into even more lurid detail of Rupert's drug addiction and violent behaviour.

"Being with me might make life more difficult. That's all," Rob finished gently.

"How can you say that? I'm not sure of many things in life, but one thing I know for certain is that I have never felt as safe and as happy as I am when I'm with you."

Rob stood up and taking her hand pulled her to her feet too.

"Then leave London to me and you go and get ready for your interview."

FOR ONCE, LUCY was ahead of schedule and thought she might actually be early for her interview until she noticed her skirt button dangling on a thread as she passed the antique mirror in the hall.

"Oh bloody hell," she cursed as she dashed into the kitchen. "Joan can you be a lifesaver and fix this button or I'll have to change my whole outfit and I'll be late."

In one smooth motion, her housekeeper put down the potato she was peeling, wiped her hands on her apron and reached for her sewing box.

"Keep still—it won't take a second—and calm down. All this dashing about can't be good for you."

Lucy had heard that tone before. "You don't approve of me standing, do you?"

"Of course I approve—my car is covered in your stickers—but I do worry you'll wear yourself out. Running this place and being an MP."

"I don't know why everyone thinks I'm going to win. Rob has even been talking about getting a place in London."

"That would be much more sensible than lots of travelling, and don't fret about this place while you're away. Bill and I will take care of things."

"I know you'll do a marvellous job, thank you." Lucy paused, wondering if she should mention something that was always in the back of her mind, but she rarely spoke about.

"And actually the more I think about having a base in London, the more I think it might be good for Freddie to get away from Hartwell."

Joan looked up at her in surprise. "Really? I can't see him taking to city life when he's used to all the freedom and space he has here."

"I know but since Sarah and her team arrived in the village, there's been a lot of talk about the curse of the Hartwell noble. As he gets older, it might be better for him to, you know, not be under its influence or whatever."

Joan tutted and shook her head. "That's a lot of old nonsense. Look at Lord Rupert. It was down in London where he got himself into the most trouble."

"I suppose so," conceded Lucy.

"And don't take my word for it—even my great-granny used to say it was a load of rubbish."

"I forgot your family were from round here. By the way, do you have a Hartwell noble?"

"I inherited one from my granny, but I haven't seen it in years. Why do you ask?"

"I was thinking about Jo. She's trying to trace her parents. The only thing she was left with was a noble. You must have seen her wearing it around her neck."

"Oh, that's right. I think I have now you mention it. Such lovely news that she and Jack are going to have a baby. She'll soon be too busy to think of anything else and sometimes the past is better left in the past."

"But do you think it means she's connected to Hartwell?"

Joan shook her head again. "Good heavens, how your

mind flits about. You've gone from London property to curses, to coins in less than five minutes."

"Don't they say a busy mind means a happy heart or something?" replied Lucy with a grin.

"No, love. They don't."

With that Joan tied off the loose thread, expertly bit through it with her teeth and sent Lucy on her way.

AS LUCY SET off to York, she checked her watch. She still had an hour before the interview, so she took a slight detour via the surgery. That morning she'd sneaked into the ball-room to check on the progress of the workmen the film company had employed. They had worked miracles. The place was beginning to look exactly as it would over two hundred years ago and it had given her an idea.

The grumpy receptionist, sitting behind the plastic screen, reluctantly told her Meera could be found in the kitchen.

"Oh hello, we don't usually see you here. Is anything wrong?" asked her friend who looked a little startled to see her. She had been staring out of the window when Lucy appeared.

"No, not at all. I have a proposition for you. How would you like to hold your wedding at Hartwell Hall?" asked Lucy, immediately. "Rob was talking to Ben in the pub and he said you'd been having difficulty finding somewhere and I know you wanted a Regency theme and I thought our ballroom would be perfect with all the work the film people are doing. It could be my wedding present to you. I've been racking my brains for what I could get you both. What do you think? Say no if you hate the idea." As usual when she was excited her words came tumbling out.

Meera stared at her for a second and her eyes began to fill with tears. Lucy was horrified.

"Oh bugger! Have I said the wrong thing? I'm so sorry. Honestly, Meera, forget I said a word."

To her great relief Meera shook her head and smiled. "Oh, Lucy, no I'm not upset. Thank you so much. The ballroom would be perfect." She reached for a tissue from her pocket and dabbed at her eyes. "I'm sorry I'm crying, but everything about the wedding seemed to be going wrong. I thought perhaps it was a sign that I was rushing into things, that it wasn't meant to be, but your offer makes everything perfect again."

Lucy clapped her hands together in glee, then hugged Meera tightly. "Oh, I'm so pleased. And not at another word about the wedding not being meant to happen. You and Ben are perfect for each other and you deserve every happiness and a fab wedding. Okay?"

"Okay," agreed Meera, but her smile had left her face again.

"Is something else up?"

"Not really. We've got Ben's mum staying with us at the moment and…well, to be honest, we aren't getting on as well as I had hoped."

Lucy couldn't comprehend anyone not getting on with kind, gentle Meera, who was always there to provide encouragement and sensible advice to her friends.

"Give it time. I'm sure she'll love you as much as we all do. Mothers-in-law can be tricky. Look at Caroline, although to be fair she's an improvement on Sadie. What I mean is, sometimes, it can take a while to get to know someone. Take your brother for example. He's been a huge help."

"What on earth is Nish helping you with?" asked Meera in surprise.

"Loads of things—printing leaflets, social media stuff. I can't think why you always say the two of you don't get on."

"We're just very different people."

"Do you think so? He reminds me of you a lot."

"Really?"

"Absolutely. You're both outgoing, helpful and friendly. He seems to know loads of people. Whenever I'm struggling to get something done, he always has a mate who can help out."

Meera smiled again. "You know the word 'mate' really doesn't suit you, Lucy."

"Oh dear, doesn't it? I was trying to sound more 'street' before my interview."

"I wouldn't bother. Be yourself and you'll have them eating out of your hand."

Lucy gave her friend another hug. "Likewise, Meera. You'll win Agnes over in no time."

DESPITE LEAVING HARTWELL in good time, Lucy hadn't accounted for how slow the traffic getting into York could be. She arrived at the radio station, breathless and with only a few minutes to spare. The radio interviewer was a serious-looking young man wearing a black polo neck and rectangular glasses. As the station didn't play pop music, Lucy wasn't familiar with him or the format of his weekly political programme.

"What would you say are your political ambitions?" was his first question.

"Oh, I don't have any," replied Lucy. "Absolutely, none. I only stood to draw attention to the lack of funding for the Rosemary Centre. It's the only place in the constituency where victims of domestic abuse can go to for help, and it has lost its funding and its home."

The interviewer gave her a quizzical look. "Isn't standing for public office a little extreme? Living at Hartwell Hall, many would see you as a wealthy individual. Wasn't there some other way of helping the centre?"

"I have offered them an empty farmhouse on the estate, but it's the day-to-day running costs that are the real issue, and unlike some charities that can rely on endowments or have funds in trust, the Rosemary Centre has been relying on funding from central government. I'd love to do more, but quite honestly all the money the estate makes goes back into maintaining it. You wouldn't believe how much it costs just to fix the roof."

"Why is the Rosemary Centre so close to your heart?"

"It's simply a wonderful place. A real haven for those who need it." As she was speaking, she caught sight of the newspaper serialising Sadie's book, folded on the desk. She had avoided reading any more. The other day, one of the men working on the ballroom had left a copy behind and

Joan had swiftly dumped it in the bin. The interviewer followed her gaze.

"Your mother, Sadie, gave an interview recently. She implied your marriage to your late husband was difficult, violent even. Is that true?"

Lucy stared across the studio at him. Despite all the warnings from Rob, Jo and the others about her personal life being under scrutiny, she hadn't imagined anyone would ask her something so direct. Although she was sure all her friends knew, she'd never spoken about life with Rupert to anyone except Sadie. She felt her heart racing and her mouth go dry, but she couldn't lose her nerve now.

"Yes, he was," she replied hearing the falter in her voice through her headphones. "That is why the Rosemary Centre is so important to me. I know exactly how the women there feel. To jump at the sound of the door, to never know whether the man walking through that door would be charming or a monster, to blame yourself. I've been in their shoes. I pretended everything was all right, I made excuses, I covered up what was happening. If I'd decided to run away, I don't know where I would have gone. That's why the Rosemary Centre is so important, and it is about time the other candidates understood that."

When she'd stopped speaking, she was amazed she wasn't crying. She actually felt incredibly calm and barely heard the interviewer when he thanked her and ended the interview.

CHAPTER TEN

L ATER THAT WEEK, Meera and Jo had arranged to meet for lunch at the White Hart. Meera had suggested it. She wanted to keep an eye on her friend, make sure she was eating properly and encourage her to attend her antenatal appointments. So far she still hadn't booked in to see the midwife. If she was honest, she also wanted an excuse not to eat at home. Agnes was still with them. After every conversation with her future mother-in-law, Meera felt like all the life had been sucked out of her.

Mealtimes were the worst. Meera had always enjoyed cooking for others, but nothing she presented Agnes with was good enough. Before even taking a bite, she would wrinkle her nose and declare it smelt too spicy and say she would prefer a sandwich in her room. The previous evening, Meera made the plainest tomato and pasta dish she could think of, only for Agnes to declare there were too many onions in it.

Ben seemed blissfully unaware of how stressed this was making Meera. All he said was: "I told you she was a fussy eater. We should have let her stay at the pub."

But Krish had picked up on the tense atmosphere at home. She had barely seen her son since Agnes had arrived.

He spent all his spare time walking the colonel's dogs or at Freddie's.

"So how are you feeling?" she asked.

"Loads better. I've finally stopped throwing up and now I'm starving all the time," said Jo, helping herself to one of the bread rolls from the basket Shirley had placed on the table.

"You look much brighter."

Jo glanced up from smearing butter on the roll. "I wish I could say the same for you. What's up? Is living with the Loch Ness monster getting to you?"

Jo had experienced one brief encounter with Agnes. After spending less than ten minutes in her company, she'd made her excuses and left, so it was clear it wasn't only Meera who Agnes upset. Ben had taken her out for supper to the White Hart to give Meera a break, but she even managed to offend the normally easy-going Shirley, by criticising the pastry in her steak and ale pie.

"You shouldn't call her that," said Meera, although she was a little relieved that she wasn't the only resident of Hartwell who found Agnes difficult.

"And you shouldn't be looking this miserable. I thought you'd be all excited about the wedding, now you've finally found a venue."

"I am. It was very kind of Lucy to offer us the ballroom. It will be absolutely perfect," replied Meera, without adding that she'd been so preoccupied with trying to please Agnes, she'd barely had time to think about her wedding.

"Hey! Nice necklace," said Jo, clocking the Hartwell noble dangling delicately around Meera's neck. She felt herself blush and touched the coin self-consciously.

"Thank you. Now we match and I feel like a real local. The colonel gave it to me. Wasn't that kind? He told me it belonged to his late wife's family."

"How's he doing?"

"He still isn't very mobile, and he's been having trouble with cooking and cleaning. I suggested he get someone in to help and he's actually employed Becky for a couple of hours every afternoon."

Jo raised her eyebrows.

"I know," continued Meera. "I was surprised too, but it actually seems to be working rather well. Apparently, he's always been a bit of a hoarder, so she's been helping him have a clear-out and organised everything, including things that belonged to his wife. It's such a shame he doesn't have any family of his own."

At that moment, Shirley arrived with their food. "It suits you love," she said nodding at Meera's noble, "and I'm sure Annabel would have approved of Hugh giving it to you. He gave me one of her watches. I have to say it made me quite emotional."

"How come they didn't have any children?" asked Jo, taking a sip of her cranberry juice.

Shirley bent down and lowered her voice. "Annabel would have loved a family, but it seems Hugh wasn't up to the job. A bout of mumps when he was a teenager left him infertile. Such a shame. They would have made wonderful parents."

"When did she die?"

"About ten years ago. Not long after Rupert's father

ironically."

"Why ironically?"

"It was assumed when they were younger that Annabel would marry Alexander Hanley. They dated as teenagers, but then Annabel met Hugh, who swept her off her feet, and it was the two of them who introduced Caroline to Alexander."

At that moment, an eighties pop tune came blaring loudly out of the stereo. Jo pulled a face.

"Jack! Turn it off!" she yelled at the same time as Shirley began to bop along in time.

"Oh, Wham! My favourite," she said as she shimmied her way back to the kitchen.

"This is why I can't move in here," muttered Jo as Jack appeared looking sheepish. "It's far too noisy for a baby."

"Sorry! I was testing out some new speakers," he apologised.

"At least your mum appreciated it," said Meera diplomatically.

"Back in the day she used to go to pop concerts with Mary, Joan, Caroline and Annabel. I think the highlight was seeing George Michael play Wembley," said Jack with a grin as he ducked back behind the bar. Meera screwed up her face.

"I really can't imagine Caroline at a pop concert." But Jo didn't appear to be listening; instead she was entering something into her phone. "What are you doing?"

"Noting down what Shirley said about the colonel's wife and reminding myself to check when George Michael played Wembley in case it tallies with when I was born. Maybe it was an excuse for one of them to be down there."

Meera looked at Jo with a mixture of sympathy and astonishment.

"You don't really think your mother could be someone you know, do you? I'm sure someone would have said something by now."

"I'm not. If anyone round here had promised to keep a secret, I think they'd take it to the grave."

"You don't know that for sure, and you never will unless you ask them outright."

"No," replied Jo firmly as she put her phone away and speared a chip with her fork, "if I've learnt one thing being in the police, it's not to start accusing someone without enough evidence. Rachel suggested I talk to the rev, but he wasn't any help. I swear he's losing the plot. I'll just have to keep digging myself."

The obstinate look on Jo's face told Meera there was no point trying to change her mind, so she decided to change the subject instead.

"I didn't know you were even considering moving in here."

Jo shrugged. "We want to live together properly when the baby arrives. There is more room here, but the cottage is more peaceful. Actually, I was hoping you might come back with me this afternoon and give me some decorating advice. We want to make the smaller bedroom into a nursery. Everyone said we should pick a neutral colour. I was going to choose green, but then Shirley said that's an unlucky colour. I picked up a colour chart and wanted to know what you thought."

"I'm sorry. I would love to help, but I can't today I'm

afraid. I promised I would drive Agnes to evensong after I leave here. Ben is on call all weekend."

"You shouldn't pander to the old bag," said Jo. "She's done nothing but complain since she got here. She's worse than Nora. Anyone normal would be thrilled to have you for a daughter-in-law, not be trying their hardest to make your life a misery."

Meera's heart began to sink as she drove back to the Grange. It had been good to catch up with Jo, but something Shirley had said about the colonel was bothering her. During one of her many attempts to find common ground with Agnes, she'd begun to discuss her work, explaining how busy they had been administering the latest Covid booster shots. Meera had thought this would be a fairly neutral subject, only for Agnes to declare firmly that she didn't believe in vaccines. At the time, Meera hadn't bothered to argue and let the matter drop. Now she wondered if Agnes hadn't vaccinated her children. Could Ben have suffered from mumps like the colonel? Was it due to Agnes, that Meera had failed to fall pregnant? One thing she did know—it wasn't going to be a conversation they would be having anytime soon.

An hour later, Meera was wrapped up in a hat and scarf, shivering outside the door of the church. Evensong was due to finish soon. Agnes had rebuffed Meera's offer to join her at the service.

"I don't think so. It wouldn't be right, seeing as you're not a believer."

Instead, Meera had paid a visit to Reverend Davenport, knowing he would be on his own while Belinda conducted the service. His ankle was much better now as he hobbled around the kitchen to make her a cup of tea, and he didn't seem quite as confused as he had been, chatting happily about village life.

"How are you settling at the Grange?" he asked as she was leaving.

"Very well, thank you. It's taken a while, but it's starting to feel like it's ours."

"Yes, so sad about the previous owner. I was trying to explain to Sergeant Ormond, only the other day. He was so very happy," he replied with a solemn shake of his head.

Meera pondered this last comment as she stood waiting for the service to finish. She'd only met Guy a few times before he'd been arrested. He'd seemed perfectly pleasant, but she wouldn't say he came across as being particularly happy. No wonder Jo had despaired with him, if he was telling her about Guy when she wanted to learn about her parents. The final note of the church organ faded away and Meera gave a sigh of relief. Despite her hat, scarf and gloves, the damp, cold evening air was making her shiver. Joan was the first of the congregation to leave. She greeted Meera with a huge smile.

"I'm so happy you'll be having your wedding at the hall," she said. "And if you need any help with the catering arrangements you only need to ask. I'd love to be involved in your big day."

Meera thanked her and watched her walk down the path to where Bill was holding the car door open, waiting to drive her home. She was such a nice woman. If she had to pick someone in the village to be Jo's mother it would be her.

"Hopefully, we'll be seeing more of you, Mrs Bannister."

Meera turned her head. Agnes and Belinda were hidden from view, but she could hear them chatting.

"I wouldn't have thought so—Inverness is a long way away."

"But the trip is surely worthwhile to see Ben and Meera. They are such a lovely couple and who knows, perhaps they may be blessed with a little one for you to visit too."

Meera smiled to herself, as Belinda echoed her own wishes, but her smile disappeared as she heard Agnes's reply.

"I don't think that would be a good idea at all. It would be far too confusing for the wee thing. It wouldn't know what it was. Good evening, Vicar."

Then Agnes stepped out of the church and with barely a nod to Meera walked straight past her and to the car. The two of them drove back to the Grange in silence. Meera felt so shocked at what she'd overheard, she couldn't bring herself to speak. They arrived back to an empty house and Agnes announced she was going upstairs to pack as she was leaving the next day. Meera went to her study, closed the door and sank down on to her chair.

On the desk in front of her were the designs for her dress and the four bridesmaids' dresses all in the empire-line style she'd carefully chosen. She scooped them up and slipped them into a drawer. Then feeling like the little girl who someone had been mean to at school, she picked up the phone and called her parents' number. As always, her mother answered.

"Oh dear, what's wrong?" she said as soon as she heard the sadness in Meera's voice. "Still not pregnant?"

Meera raised her eyes to the ceiling. Her mother took

being direct to a new level.

"No and I might never be. I'm worried Ben might have had mumps. I don't think Agnes vaccinated him when he was little. What if that means we can't have children?" replied Meera, the stress of the last few days making her feel close to tears. "It feels like the universe is telling me to slow down. That I'm trying to move too quickly."

"For heaven's sake, Meera. You could be worrying pointlessly. Remember what we said? No more secrets. Why don't you ask Ben or his mother outright?"

"I don't really think I can discuss this with Agnes." Then in a shaking voice, she told her mother what she'd overheard. There was a heavy sigh at the end of the line.

"At least now you know why she has been so unpleasant to you."

"You don't think I misunderstood then?" asked Meera without much hope.

"No, I don't, darling and if the universe is telling you anything, it's that your future mother-in-law is a racist. You need to say something to her and to Ben. Stand up for yourself."

Meera put the phone down. She knew her mother was right. Only a few days ago she had told Krish the same. However, it was one thing to stand up to Nora, but what was she meant to say to the woman who had raised the man she loved?

Chapter Eleven

T HE VILLAGE HALL was packed. The parish council were holding a meeting to decide on the proposal to turn the Foxton farm buildings into a centre for Celtic heritage and Rachel had made sure as many of her friends and relatives as possible were there. Sarah was standing at the front of the hall, and she was almost at the end of her presentation. She had been planning it for weeks, rehearsing every word and slide in their sitting room. Rachel had found it fascinating, and it would probably have gone down a storm in one of Sarah's lectures, but tonight it seemed she might have misjudged her audience.

Rachel glanced around nervously. Caroline was making notes and Meera was smiling and nodding politely, but Sarah was in danger of losing the rest of the room. The colonel, who had arrived on crutches, was looking bored. Reverend Davenport had already dozed off, Jack was trying unsuccessfully to stifle a yawn, while Lucy kept trying to discreetly check her phone. Dan's eyes had glazed over, and he and her uncle Frank were both shifting uncomfortably in their seats. Sarah finally got to her last slide and sat down to subdued applause. She looked across to Rachel, who gave her the most encouraging smile she could muster.

The colonel, who was chair of the council, rose to his feet, wincing slightly. "Thank you, Professor Stevenson. That was most informative. Are there any questions?"

There was an awkward silence as the colonel waited and Sarah sat up eagerly.

"Very well," continued the colonel when nobody raised their hand. "Would anyone like to speak against the proposal?" she asked.

Rachel had to stop herself rolling her eyes as predictably Nora stood up, full of self-importance.

"I for one, certainly object," she began. "One of my shop storerooms backs on to the Foxton farm buildings. I'm not at all sure I or my customers would like the thought of skeletons being only inches away from my tinned goods."

"For heaven's sake!" protested Rachel. "You've got the graveyard on the other side of the shop. What's the difference?"

"That's consecrated ground. The people there are laid to rest in a proper Christian way."

Sarah stood up to speak again. "Let me reassure you, Mrs Parkin, there will only be animal bones on display. We have discovered several that have been intricately carved and will be shown alongside pieces of jewellery we have discovered too. All human remains will be reinterred where we found them, and we have even arranged for a Druid priest to conduct a burial ceremony."

This bit of news caused a stir of excitement around the room, but Nora still wasn't mollified.

"I don't like the sound of that. Pagans in the village. What if all this digging up reawakens the curse? Why should we risk that for the sake of some museum?"

A few of the older, more superstitious residents were nodding in agreement and Rachel could see Sarah beginning to look nervous as she stood up to reply again.

"I understand your fears and the history of the curse is something my team and I will be focusing our research on next. Hopefully, what we discover will allay any concerns, but if I am correct and there is a curse, it only applied to the Hanley family, not the village of Hartwell. Isn't that right?"

She turned to Rachel for support, who feeling guilty, could only nod her head. There was another murmur around the room. All eyes switched to Lucy, who had turned quite pale. Rachel knew how much she hated any talk about the supposed curse. Joan, who was sitting next to her, had placed a reassuring arm around her shoulder. Nora looked like she was about to speak again, but the colonel raised his hand.

"Nora! I would prefer it if we focused on the proposal instead of all this curse mumbo jumbo. Rachel, I assume you are speaking in support of the proposal?"

Rachel shifted uncomfortably under the colonel and the rest of the council's gaze. She hadn't planned on saying anything, but she couldn't risk Sarah's proposal being turned down. Rising to her feet, she cleared her throat.

"Yes, I am," she declared sounding more confident than she felt.

"Oh, what a surprise!" scoffed Nora.

"Since meeting Professor Stevenson, I've learnt so much about the history and heritage of our wonderful village."

"You've changed your tune. For years you've been harping on about going travelling, wanting to get away from here," heckled Nora again.

Rachel turned to her. "Well, I was wrong, and those of you here who know me, know how much I hate admitting that."

A chuckle went round the room.

"I have lived here all my life and I took Hartwell for granted. It took, Sarah, Professor Stevenson, a newcomer to open my eyes to how special this place is." She glanced across to where several of the older farmers were congregated. With their arms folded across their chests, they still looked sceptical. "But if we want the village to thrive, we need to let others know how special Hartwell is too. It's no secret that traditional farming is getting more and more difficult. We need to diversify. Look at what Lucy, is doing up at the Hall. How many of us here are already branching out into tourism, offering bed and breakfast, or converting old barns into holiday cottages, turning fields into campsites. By making Hartwell into a centre of Celtic history, we could attract even more visitors, from international scholars to school children. That would benefit all of us. Everyone from the pub to the village shop."

"Hear! Hear!" called out Jack.

"That's all we need—a bunch of inner-city delinquents running amok all over the place!" grumbled Nora, but Rachel ignored her. The majority of the room were slowly nodding their heads in agreement. It looked like she might have won them over. The colonel, who was clearly impatient for the meeting to be over, put the proposal to a vote and it was passed unanimously. Permission was granted and greeted by a small cheer from Jack and a sigh of relief from Rachel.

As soon as the meeting was adjourned, she hurried over to congratulate Sarah, who was looking slightly shell-shocked.

"I really thought they were going to turn me down. Thank you so much for what you said."

Rachel wrapped her arms around her and hugged her tight. "Don't be silly. We're in this together. A team, remember?" she said.

"Drinks at the Hart to celebrate?" Jack called over.

Rachel gave him a thumbs up. "We'll be right there—I just want to check Lucy is okay. She looked upset when the curse was mentioned." But as she looked around she realised Lucy and Joan had already left. "Maybe we can catch up with her at the pub. Let me give you a hand?" she said to Sarah who was packing away her laptop.

"No it's fine. You go ahead without me."

Rachel looked at her in surprise. "Don't you want to come? I really think we should thank everyone who came to the meeting for their support."

"You'll be better at that than me. Besides, I want to get all this equipment safely back to the cottage."

"Okay. If you're sure. I'll only stay for a couple."

Sarah nodded, but as Rachel walked out of the village hall, she couldn't help feeling the sense of celebration had fallen a bit flat.

The next morning, the two of them were both up early. Sarah wanted to drive through to York and share the good news in person with the rest of her team, and Rachel needed to go for a long run. The calories in all those glasses of wine she'd drunk in celebration were bound to appear on her stomach if she didn't.

An hour later she returned to the cottage. Hot and sweating, she went straight to the kitchen and filled a glass from the tap. She took a long drink then paused when she heard a knock at the front door. Still glugging down water, Rachel went to answer it and almost choked to find Caroline standing there. The dowager Lady Hanley rarely deigned to visit anyone. If she wanted to see you, you were usually summoned.

"Hello, Caroline, would you like to come in? Can I get you a cup of tea or coffee?"

Caroline stepped through the door into the cottage's sitting room. "No thank you. This isn't a social call. I want to talk to you about the parish council."

"I thought the proposal was carried. Is there a problem?" asked Rachel, suddenly feeling worried.

"No. There isn't a problem. I thought you spoke very well last night. Clear, concise and to the point."

Rachel was momentarily stunned. A compliment from Caroline was even rarer than a visit.

"I want to discuss the council itself," Caroline continued. "I think it's about time you took a more active role. There has been a vacancy for some time now, and it can't have escaped your notice the colonel and I aren't getting any younger. At some point in the future, there will need to be a new chair. Who better than a Foxton?"

Rachel shook her head. "You want me to join the council? I'm sorry, I really don't think I have the time."

Caroline gave her a withering looking. "Don't be ridiculous—you must find the time. As you said last night, you now finally appreciate how special Hartwell is. The community here has always supported you and your family. Don't you think it's about time to give something back? I heard Sergeant Ormond use an interesting phrase the other day: 'to put your money where your mouth is'. I rather like it."

"Even if I was to stand, there is no guarantee anyone would vote for me," protested Rachel. She was treated to a second look of disdain.

"Please don't make excuses, Rachel. There has been a vacancy since the last election—we can have you co-opted. I have already discussed it with the other members."

Without waiting for a reply, Caroline headed back to the door.

Rachel hurried after her. "All this talk of elections. Sleepy old Hartwell is turning into a bit of a political hotbed, isn't it?" she said weakly, trying to delay Caroline as she struggled to think if there was any way she could get out of this predicament.

Caroline paused at the door and turned to look at Rachel. Her expression was inscrutable. "I never really understood the friendship between yourself and Lucinda, but perhaps you are more alike than I realised."

AFTER CAROLINE HAD gone, Rachel quickly showered then went to visit her mother.

"Oh dear, what's the long face for?" asked Mary as soon as Rachel walked into the farmhouse kitchen.

"Caroline wants me to join the parish council."

"That's nice."

"No, it isn't! I'll be bored out of my mind. It will take up loads of time and I'm going to be busy enough with the heritage centre."

"Your father would have been very proud."

Rachel couldn't argue with this. Her dad had been a councillor himself, before his accident, and she knew her mother was right—he would want another Foxton to represent the village. There was no point in complaining any more. She sat down at the pine kitchen table and reached for a piece of shortbread, still warm from the oven.

"It's very quiet. Where are Becky and Minty?"

"Over at the colonel's. Becky's been doing some cleaning and cooking for him. She's been helping him sort the place out too. The other day she found a doll's house in one of the bedrooms. It had been Annabel's when she was a little girl. The colonel had forgotten all about it. He thought Minty might like to play with it. Between you and me, I think he gets a bit lonely."

Rachel nodded, but privately wondered how much help her undomesticated sister could really be.

WHEN SARAH RETURNED home later that day, she found Rachel poring over the local government website.

"What are you doing?"

"Caroline bamboozled me this morning. She roped me into joining the parish council."

Sarah grimaced. "Poor you! I certainly don't envy you if last night was anything to go by. Can't you get out of it?"

"She laid a guilt trip on me and then Mum joined in, telling me how proud Dad would have been. I hate to admit it but she might have a point. I'm the first to complain when I think the council has done something stupid. Rather than complaining, maybe it's time I got involved, like Lucy is doing with the Rosemary Centre."

Sarah turned away and Rachel decided to shut up. Lucy was still a prickly subject as far as Sarah was concerned and everything between them was going so well, she didn't want to spoil it.

CHAPTER TWELVE

J O WAS STARING out of the office window, giving her eyes a rest from looking at the computer screen. She took another bite out of an apple. Now that the horrendous sickness had finally subsided, she was trying to take better care of herself. Looking down on to the car park her eyes rested on a dark grey Audi with London plates. She knew that car. It belonged to Seb Devizes, one of the other candidates in the election.

When Guy was first arrested, he'd been a regular visitor to the station. Officially, as one of Guy's advisers, he was there to assist the police, but Jo had always got the feeling he was spying on them. She had a sneaking suspicion he might be behind the nasty story about Rob having been in prison that had appeared in the local newspaper a couple of days ago. Not that it seemed to have made any difference—Lucy was still only a couple of points behind him in the opinion polls. What was he doing here today though?

Suddenly she was disturbed by the noisy roar of a car engine. She flicked her eyes to the car park entrance where an all too familiar black BMW came hurtling through. She'd always thought you could tell a lot about a person by the way they drove a car. Rachel who had grown up driving tractors was calm, capable and unshowy. Meera was super safe, with her hands at ten and two on the steering wheel and constantly checking her mirrors. Jo had vowed never to get in a car Lucy was driving. She was far too easily distracted by trying to find a song she liked on the radio or swerving all over the road to avoid hitting a pheasant.

The BWM below shrieked to a halt before executing a perfect handbrake turn into the space next to Devizes's car. Out stepped DS Simon Spencer in his sunglasses and leather jacket.

"Wow!" exclaimed Dawson who had appeared next to her, his mouth wide open.

"All style and no substance," muttered Jo as she turned away. Now there was another unwelcome visitor from London to contend with. He must be here about the guns. Jo had reported that Caroline had sent them to the auction house without informing either Rupert or Lucy. Surely he couldn't still think there was a connection with his case and Hartwell.

Half an hour later, she was summoned to the chief constable's office, who told her that was exactly why he was here.

"DS Spencer will be spending the next couple of weeks with us. I understand the two of you know each other already, so working together shouldn't be a problem."

"No, sir," agreed Jo reluctantly. As much as she wanted to get back to London, she really couldn't see there being a connection between Hartwell and the two armed robbers. She also felt very uneasy about Spencer poking around in the Hanley file. It wasn't simply another case to her. If he started asking awkward questions it could affect Lucy and Rachel.

She trudged away from his office and was so deep in thought, she almost bumped into Devizes.

"Good morning, Sergeant Ormond," he said.

"What brings you here?" she replied.

"I wanted to check everything is in order for poor old Guy's trial. As I'm sure you know it starts very soon. Although he won't be there in person, we want to make sure he gets a fair hearing."

"Yeh right," muttered Jo sarcastically. 'Poor old Guy'! That's how his team had been spinning the case. Making out he was an overworked civil servant who had acted out of character due to pressure, not that he was an out-of-control psycho. She began to walk away, but he called after her.

"I expect your friend, Lady Hanley, will be pleased to put all this unpleasantness behind her, especially with the election so close. It's a pity you didn't find more evidence during your search of the Grange. Something that could have helped."

Jo looked over her shoulder and scowled. She was sure he had been to the Grange before them and removed anything incriminating. No doubt, if challenged, he would deny it or say he was acting in the interests of national security. He had, however, left behind the photos of Lucy arguing with Rupert on the night he disappeared. Jo had given these photos to Lucy rather than including them with the rest of the evidence.

Devizes gave her his most condescending smile. "I'm pleased to see she is coping so well with all the press attention. An attractive young widow is bound to make the front pages. There are very few people who can handle that level of interest in their private lives. She's lucky to have a friend like you to support her."

Jo didn't bother to reply, but continued on her way, swearing under her breath. She found Spencer in the canteen regaling Dawson and some of the uniforms with an exaggerated story of how he was stabbed while arresting an infamous drug dealer.

Jo rolled her eyes. "Give it a rest, Si. It was barely a scratch," she interrupted loudly.

He turned round to look at her and grinned. "There you are, Jo. I hear congratulations are in order. I have to say, I never had you down as the maternal type."

Jo scowled at Dawson. Trust him to blab. Her deputy looked contrite as she turned her attention back to Simon.

"You're wasting your time up here. I'm telling there is no way your two guys were involved with what happened to Rupert."

"Maybe, maybe not, but I've been reading the notes on the Hanley case, and something doesn't add up. Palmer agrees with me. It'll be good to work with you again."

He held out his hand and not wanting to look childish in front of the others, Jo shook it, then turned to go. The last thing she or Lucy and Rachel needed was him getting involved in what they all thought was a closed investigation. Why couldn't he and Devizes just sod off back to London?

She was almost out of the door when suddenly everything went black. The next thing she knew she was on the floor with Dawson holding her hand and shouting her name.

Jo LAY ON the bed trying not to think how desperately she needed the loo. After her fainting episode, Meera had checked her over and arranged for Jo to have a scan.

"I'm sure everything is fine, although your blood pressure is a little low, but a scan will help put your mind at rest," Meera had said in her most reassuring voice.

Jack was sitting next to her, squeezing her hand so tightly it was starting to tingle. He'd been a nervous wreck since Dawson had called him to come and collect her. She'd refused to let anyone phone an ambulance. Jack had flinched when she'd explained she'd fainted after talking to Spencer.

"What's he doing up here?" he'd asked.

"Getting in the way mainly," she'd replied, then seeing his face: "Don't look like that. If it wasn't for him, we might not have got together. He won't be staying long. There's nothing for him here." Since then neither of them had mentioned her ex.

Now Jack was squinting at the screen while the radiologist slowly moved the scanner across her gel-covered stomach. Jo wasn't looking at the screen. Her eyes were firmly fixed on the young woman's face. There was no way she would ever be able to make sense of the shadowy blobs on the screen but she could read faces. Years of interviewing suspects had taught her to look out for a jaw tightening, a flicker of an eyelid or a nervous lick of the lips. The smallest sign could reveal that things weren't going well, but the woman's expression did not change.

"Is everything all right?" asked Jack for what seemed like the tenth time.

"Everything looks good," the radiologist repeated yet

again.

Jack bent down and planted a kiss on her forehead.

"Can you tell if it's a boy or a girl?" he asked turning back to the radiologist.

"Do you want to know?" she asked looking at them both. Jo shrugged. She was still struggling to get her head around the fact she was going to have a baby, let alone whether it would be a boy or a girl.

"Congratulations. You're having a little girl."

"Really? That's fantastic. A beautiful baby girl. She's going to be just like you," said Jack.

"Are you sure you can handle two of us? I thought you'd want a boy to pass all your rugby and cricket skill on to."

"I can still do that with a girl. All that matters is that she is healthy."

"You are sure she is?" asked Jo.

The radiologist nodded. "Yes."

Jo let her head fall back, closed her eyes and exhaled loudly. It felt like she'd been holding her breath since she arrived at the hospital.

"Are you okay?" asked Jack urgently.

"I need the loo. Can I go now?"

"Yes, of course it's halfway down the corridor. I'll print out the results while we wait for you to come back."

Jack drove the two of them back to Hartwell. He chattered away excitedly, as she closed her eyes and listened to him. The black-and-white grainy image was lying on her knee. Meera had been right—having the scan had put her mind at rest and made it all feel a bit more real. Up until now, a little bit of her hadn't quite believed it was possible she was having a baby. Now she knew it wasn't just a baby, but a little girl.

"Do you want to put your feet up and I'll fix you something to eat?" he asked as they arrived back at the cottage.

"No thanks. I think I'll take Baxter for a walk. I could do with some fresh air. I've still got that horrible hospital smell in my nostrils."

"Are you sure you'll be okay? He can pull a bit."

Jo gave him a warning look and thankfully he shut up. She handed the image from the scan to him. "I'll be fine. Why don't you go and tell Shirley that everything is okay and that she's going to have a granddaughter, and I'll see if I can hear the shouts of excitement from this end of the village."

She and Baxter walked towards Hartwell Hall. A cold wind blew against her face, but she didn't care. She needed to be alone, to let the news she was having a daughter sink. As much as she adored Jack, she couldn't think properly when he was talking constantly. Had her own mother known she was having a daughter? Did they even scan pregnant women back then?

Since finding out she was pregnant, her own feelings had fluctuated between panic, fear and confusion. Obsessing about who her mother might be had been a distraction, something for her to focus on even if Jack had started saying she was 'clutching at straws'. Today was the first time she'd allowed herself to feel a little bit of excitement. The radiologist had said her baby girl was healthy. Now that she knew that, did it really matter if she found her mother? After all, if she was here in Hartwell, it was obvious she had no intention of revealing herself. Perhaps it was time to look to the future and not the past.

She was suddenly jolted back to reality. Baxter was indeed pulling on his lead, so she let the eager Labrador off when they reached the woods. Above her head the bare branches creaked and groaned in the wind. She trudged along as Baxter bounded ahead through the oak trees to the ancient well. She had expected to be alone and was a little surprised to find someone else already resting on the edge of the stone wall that ran around the well. Colonel Marsden slowly rose to his feet when he saw her approach. His three dogs, who were waiting obediently by his feet, gave Baxter a look of haughty disdain as he sniffed them enthusiastically in greeting.

"Hello there, how are you feeling?" she asked.

"Mustn't grumble. Still not back up to my usual speed, but at least I've got rid of those damn crutches."

There was a sudden cacophony of shrieks and calls as the wood's rooks came home to roost. Dusk was beginning to fall.

The colonel looked up. "Noisy blighters, aren't they? They remind me of the ravens at the Tower."

"The Tower of London?"

"That's right. It must be about thirty years ago now. I was in post there for six years. Annabel loved it. All those smart shops practically on our doorstep and being able to hop on a train at Kings Cross and head back up to Yorkshire. Her parents were still alive then of course, but her mother wasn't well. She spent as much time up here as she could. Previously, we'd been stationed in the Falklands, so it was quite a change." He seemed lost in his thoughts for a moment.

"I hear she grew up here."

"Yes. Hartwell born and bred. She loved this place. Would always come to this old well and make a wish. Even after that poor chap died here. It never seemed to put her off."

"Which poor chap?"

"I forget his name. An archaeologist. Interested in Druids and Celts rather like Professor Stevenson."

"You mean the guy buried in the church yard? He killed himself here?"

"That's right. Bullet to the head. Bit thoughtless if you ask me. A youngster could have stumbled across him, but then I expect he wasn't thinking straight. Turned out he was found by an eager young police constable, who suspected foul play. Wishful thinking on his part perhaps. Anyway, I must be going. I tend to stiffen up if I stand still for too long. Good to see you, Sergeant." With a friendly salute he slowly walked away accompanied by his canine companions.

Jo watched him go. She had the strangest feeling he'd told her something important.

CHAPTER THIRTEEN

L UCY DROVE BACK towards the village. She'd been up to
Moorhead Farm. Alison had met her there with an
architect to discuss the Rosemary Centre using it as their new
home. Thanks to all the publicity she had generated, the
charity had more than enough to do the necessary work to
make the place habitable again. Her radio interview in
particular had resulted in a huge spike in donations. Unfortunately, there still hadn't been any movement on the
promise of funding for the annual running costs. Meanwhile,
she and Devizes were now neck and neck in the polls.

Bumping along the narrow country lanes in Dizzy, her
ancient Land Rover, she kept having to break and swerve for
the pheasants who seemed to be playing a particularly
reckless game of chicken with her. It was late November.
Even at this time of year, when the trees were bare and the
fields were empty and brown, she still thought the countryside looked beautiful. After several days of rain, the sun was
making a rare appearance and the land was dappled brown,
green and purple in its light.

She'd fallen in love with Hartwell and the moors that
rose up behind it the first time Rupert had brought her up
here. Until then, she'd always thought of herself as a city girl,

born and raised in London. If by any miracle, she did manage to win this election, she would be spending a lot more time back down there. The idea seemed crazy, but recently she'd been wondering if it could be fate giving her a nudge. Since the council meeting when she'd sat in the audience and listened to Sarah speak, she'd been worrying more than usual about Freddie. Despite Joan's reassurances, perhaps a move away from Hartwell would be the best for both of them. As much as she loved Hartwell, she loved Freddie more.

For once she wasn't listening to pop music as she drove along but had instead retuned the radio to the local station that had interviewed her. They were also interviewing the other candidates. Today, it was Heather Rhodes's turn. She sounded calmer and more measured than when she'd spoken at the hustings. Lucy had to admit she had some excellent ideas and policies, especially when it came to education and the environment. Suddenly, she heard the interviewer mention her own name and she turned up the volume.

"Lucy Hanley one of the other candidates was on this programme a few days ago. Although you are trailing her in the polls, if you were to win, can you promise that you will also campaign for the Rosemary Centre?"

"Yes, I would," replied Heather immediately. "I have spent time at the Rosemary Centre volunteering and learning about the valuable work they do. If I may, I would like to publicly thank Lucy for drawing my attention to this important charity."

"Yes!" said Lucy quietly raising a clenched fist in triumph. Finally, she had won one of her opponents over. Only three more to go. Although to be honest, Devizes was the only one who really counted and she doubted he would ever change his mind.

As she entered the village, she spotted Jo, who had been signed off work since her fainting episode. She was balancing a bike with one hand and holding on to a panting Baxter with the other. Lucy beeped her horn, pulled up on the cobbles and wound down the car window.

"Hello, you two! You look much better. I told you the morning sickness doesn't last forever."

"Now I just have stretch marks and the pain of childbirth to look forward to."

"Honestly, I know you might not feel this way right now, but I promise it's all worth it."

"I hope so. I've even had to abandon running and switch to cycling. Although Shirley's bike is so knackered, I may as well walk."

"It won't be forever and I hear you're having a little girl too. How exciting is that? I think between them Shirley, Mary and Joan might have cornered the market in pink wool. She'll be the best dressed baby in North Yorkshire."

Jo shook her head. "You're right. It is an exciting time. Shirley has gone completely overboard and dyed her hair the colour of bubble gum. Ignore me, Lucy. I'm in a bad mood. Meera got me one of those gadgets to keep checking my blood pressure at home, but it's still low. I thought it was high blood pressure that was bad." She sighed again. "I've never been off work this long before. I don't know what to do with myself. I keep biting Jack's head off. He let Baxter raid the bins again and I yelled at him that he's going to need to be more responsible when he's a father."

Lucy gave her a sympathetic look. "Don't worry about Jack. You could literally bite his head off and he would still adore you."

Baxter woofed in agreement and Jo finally smiled too.

"How about you? How's the campaign going?" she asked nodding at the 'Vote Hanley' stickers covering Dizzy.

"I'm really enjoying it," admitted Lucy. "I was canvassing in Thirsk yesterday. You know how I love to chat to people and everyone seemed really friendly. More importantly the Rosemary Centre has now got enough money to move to Moorhead Farm."

"Sounds like politics could be your calling. And I guess, being so busy you haven't had time to worry about the court case."

Lucy glanced away. It was true—she'd been trying not to think about the trial against Guy that was due to start in a few days.

"Will you be there?" she asked.

"Yes, I've been called to give evidence as the arresting officer. Even if they have to wheel me in, I'll be there." She paused. "I might not be in the courtroom at the same time as you though. It depends on what order they call us to give evidence. Sorry."

"I know. It's okay. It's the same with the other witnesses—Joan, Rob and Jack—but Rachel and Meera said they will try to take time off work so at least there should be a couple of friendly faces."

"You needn't think I'll be wasting my vote on you!"

Lucy and Jo both turned to see Nora, standing with her

sweeping brush outside the village shop.

"You can bet she'll be on the front row in court," muttered Jo.

Lucy grimaced before calling out, "Sorry to hear that, Mrs Parkin. Of course you must choose whomever you think is best." Then lowering her voice: "I'm not getting into a political discussion with her. I'll see you later, Jo."

She drove farther through the village and stopped outside the village hall. Her poster had been removed, from the noticeboard, no doubt by Nora. She got out to replace it and was sticking in the last drawing pin, when Caroline stepped out of the village hall.

"Ah, Lucinda. I've been meaning to talk to you." Lucy felt her heart sink. "I noticed Dr Kumar's brother driving around in one of the estate vehicles. Have you employed him?"

"No. At least not exactly." Lucinda sighed, knowing Caroline was bound to be annoyed she'd involved Nish in estate business without her prior approval, but she may as well get it over with. "He's been helping me with my campaign, and he's helped me find people who want to use the estate for music videos and photo shoots. He's got a lot of contacts in Leeds and Bradford. Musicians, artists, those sorts of people."

"That sounds very much like the work of an estate manager. I hope you haven't employed him without consulting me or the rest of the board of directors?"

"I haven't employed him," explained Lucy patiently. She noted Caroline ignored the mention of her campaign. Her mother-in-law had already declared her decision to stand for election as 'utter folly'. "Nish hasn't got a contract as such—he's working on commission. If he doesn't bring any bookings, he doesn't get paid. It seemed more sensible than having someone employed full-time with all the extra costs that incurs."

"Does he know anything about estate management?" persisted Caroline. "What qualifications does he hold? All our previous agents went to Cirencester."

"Including Max and look how that turned out," retorted Lucy. "The estate is moving in a different direction, and I think Nish is exactly what we need, even if he doesn't have lots of qualifications."

Caroline pursed her lips. "On the subject of education, have you filled in the application form I sent you for Darkwood College?"

"No." Lucy took a deep breath. She really didn't have the time for an argument with her mother-in-law, but there was no point in putting off this conversation any longer. "And I'm not planning to. I don't want Freddie to go there."

"The Hanleys have been educated at Darkwood for generations."

"I know, but forgive me for saying this, Caroline, I don't think they turned out all that well."

Caroline opened her mouth, but Lucy was determined to say her piece without interruption. "In a year or so, I may look at the independent schools in York, but Freddie will not be boarding. He would hate it and so would I."

Caroline raised her eyebrows. "It does us good to face our fears. Many people see boarding school as character-building. I can't help feeling he'll have a rather sheltered upbringing if he never leaves Yorkshire," she said.

"I'm not saying he'll never leave Yorkshire. Who knows, if by some miracle I win this election, we might both move to London. Rob is already looking at houses down there."

Caroline's mouth fell open and for once she seemed lost for words. "You'd leave Hartwell?" she almost choked.

Lucy shrugged. "Perhaps—who knows what the future holds, but I do know it will be a joint decision between me and my son. No one else."

"I see. Well, you have made it very clear that my opinion is unwanted and my feelings are to be disregarded. Good day."

She turned on her heel and marched back towards the dower house. Lucy watched her go. At one time she would have called out or gone after her, tried to make amends, but not anymore. She wasn't only tired of being scared, she was tired of being pushed around too.

LATER THAT EVENING, Lucy was curled up with Rob on the sofa in the library. She had barely stopped all day. Meeting Nish's DJ friend, checking on the progress in the ballroom and doing a telephone interview with a local newspaper. Now they were watching the news on the television. The reporter was discussing the by-election and there had been a brief mention of Guy's trial.

"You're very quiet. Are you thinking about the court case?" asked Rob as he stroked her hair.

"A bit, but actually there's something else that's been

bothering me. I've been thinking a lot about what you said about getting a place in London. I know we talked about getting a little pad to crash at and you offered to stay up here with Freddie and take care of things while I was away, but perhaps a move to London might be best for all of us."

Rob looked at her incredulously. "Are you serious? Leave Hartwell? After all the hard work you've put into making the estate profitable, preserving it for Freddie's future? Why would you want to leave?"

"Promise you won't laugh." She paused. "I've been thinking recently about the Hartwell curse."

Rob leaned back against the sofa and groaned loudly.

"No, listen. I know you think it's nonsense, but hear me out. At the village hall meeting, Sarah was talking about the nobles and how the curse is meant to apply to the Hanley family. She's an academic, and she was taking it seriously. What if there is some truth in it? None of the Hanley men seem to have had very happy lives. Most have died before their time and to put it mildly they all sound like a bunch of rogues. Perhaps it would be better for Freddie to grow up away from here. We could put Rupert, Guy, everything that has happened behind us. If I do win the by-election, maybe it's fate's way of telling me he should grow up somewhere else. I know you'll say I'm being silly, but I can't help the way I feel."

Rob stared at her for a moment, then he sat up and took Lucy's face in his hands.

"Look at me, Lucy. If you want to live in London, or Timbuktu or anywhere else, that's fine by me. I'd live in a tent with you and Freddie in the middle of nowhere if it made you happy, but don't base your decision on some stupid curse. If most of the Hanley men had rotten lives and died early, it's because they were rotten bastards, spoilt and entitled and no doubt got everything they deserved. Freddie is a good kid. I remember Rupert at his age and he was totally different. He was mean and selfish even then. You are an amazing mother, and you are raising a great son and no Druid curse on a few old coins is going to change that."

Lucy opened her mouth to reply, but Rob—who normally never used two words when one would do—hadn't finished.

"Why not talk to Freddie? He loves living here. I can't see him wanting to swap the freedom of roaming around hundreds of acres with his dogs for life in a big city."

As if on cue, Freddie appeared in the doorway. "What are you two talking about? You both look really serious."

Rob gave Lucy a meaningful look.

"We were just talking about living in London if I won the election."

Freddie frowned at her. She thought he suddenly looked very grown-up.

"I thought Rob and I were going to stay up here with the dogs, and you would go down during the week."

"Well, yes that was the original idea. Wouldn't you like to live in London?"

Freddie shook his head firmly. "No way! I mean I like the Natural History Museum and I wouldn't mind seeing the Tower of London, at least the bit where they chopped people's heads off, but you can't live in either of those places, can you? I mean not unless you are someone like the colonel."

"No, you can't," admitted Lucy, trying to ignore Rob's 'I told you so' face.

"Besides," added Freddie as he knelt down to ruffle Roots' ears, "the dogs would hate London."

"That settles it. You've been outvoted, five to one," whispered Rob.

A FEW DAYS later, Lucy took her seat in the witness box. She glanced up to the public gallery. Jo gave her an encouraging smile. As the arresting officer, she had given her evidence that morning. Lucy's eyes drifted along the rest of the gallery. Jo was the only person there that she recognised. Meera had promised to try to make it in time, but she was working that morning, as was Rachel. Joan and Jack had wanted to be there for her, but they were being called as witnesses the next day. It was the same with Rob, who was waiting for her outside.

Her eyes suddenly stopped on a familiar, but unwelcome face. Seb Devizes was sitting in the far corner of the gallery, looking bored. What on earth was he doing here? Their eyes suddenly met, and Lucy quickly looked away and gave the clerk of the court her full attention. She could hear her voice trembling as she confirmed her name.

"You have stated that you viewed the accused as a friend. Is that correct?" asked the defence barrister. A tall, thin man, who Lucy suspected might be bald beneath his grey wig.

"Yes," she replied, remembering to keep her answers

short and to the point as Jo had told her.

"A close friend?" pressed the barrister.

"Yes."

"The two of you would often socialise, go for a drink together."

"Sometimes."

"You trusted him. You would go to him for advice, seek out his opinion."

"Yes," replied Lucy. Her palms had become sweaty while her mouth felt as dry as sand.

"I'm sure he was very flattered," commented the defence, arching an eyebrow.

"Objection," snapped the prosecution barrister, who was watching their exchange like a hawk.

"Withdrawn, your honour," the defence barrister replied before the judge could direct him to, then he turned his attention back to Lucy. "You encouraged this close friendship between yourself and the accused, even though your husband was still presumed to be alive at the time. Would you say you gave the impression of being a single woman?"

The prosecution barrister leapt to her feet. "Objection. The witness is not on trial, your honour."

The judge leaned forward slightly and peered over the top of her glasses. "Sustained. Move on, please."

HALF AN HOUR later, with a huge sense of relief Lucy left the witness box and stepped outside to where Jo and a slightly out of breath Meera were waiting for her.

"I'm so sorry I wasn't here in time. How was it?" asked Meera.

"Pretty tough," admitted Lucy.

Jo snorted. "The defence barrister was a complete bastard. He should be struck off."

Lucy shook her head. "He was only doing his job, and do you want to know something? It was terrifying, but I actually found it quite therapeutic. All the questions he asked, they were only the same ones I'd asked myself. Wondering if Guy's behaviour was somehow my fault, if I'd encouraged him."

Meera began to protest, but Lucy held up her hands.

"It's okay, I know it wasn't me, but him. But I do think sometimes women blame themselves. It was the same with Rupert. I used to think if I was more interesting or sexier, he would change. I hear similar stories from the women at the Rosemary Centre."

At that moment, Rob came hurrying towards them. He scooped Lucy up in his arms and held her tight.

"I'm sorry I wasn't here. I only went outside for a second to take a call. Rachel wanted to know what was happening. Are you okay? What did they ask?"

"I'm fine," she assured him. "It wasn't any worse than I was expecting. The good news is the court has adjourned for the day so we can go home."

"Great the pickup is parked outside."

"I'll meet you out there. I just want to nip to the loo," said Lucy.

"We'll see you back in Hartwell," Meera called after her as she and Jo turned to leave.

In the ladies', Lucy washed her hands and reapplied the lipstick she'd nervously licked off. Staring at her reflection she took a deep breath. She'd been dreading today, but now it was over with. Time to put it behind her and move on. She left the cloakroom and started scrolling through her messages. She was about to turn down the corridor that led back to the car park, when she noticed a dark figure standing in her way.

"Good afternoon, Lady Hanley," said Seb Devizes giving her one of his superior smiles. "I do hope today hasn't been too stressful for you."

"Thank you. It's over now and I seem to have survived," she replied briskly. She tried to get past him, but he blocked her again.

"Indeed. In fact, you seem to be thriving with all this attention you're receiving. Some might say you enjoy publicity as much as your mother. No wonder you decided to stand for election."

"I'm not doing this for myself but for the Rosemary Centre."

"You have such noble intentions. It would be a shame if you suffered because of them." He reached into the breast pocket of his immaculate suit and produced two black-and-white images. She knew them well. They showed her arguing with Rupert on the night he disappeared. In one of them she was holding a spade above her head.

"Snap," she said. "I have the same at home."

She couldn't believe how calm she sounded. Inside her heart was racing and her stomach was churning. She noticed Seb blink twice. Her reaction obviously wasn't what he was expecting either.

"I did wonder if Sergeant Ormond would pass on the copies we left behind at the Grange. Could that be seen as tampering with evidence, a dereliction of duty perhaps? I'd be interested to hear what the chief constable has to say on the matter."

"Then ask him. I'm sure he'd want to know why you have them too. As for Jo, she's a big girl. She can take care of herself," replied Lucy, wishing very much that her bolshie, tough friend was with her right now.

"Perhaps, but you do see how your actions may affect those you care about? If these photos were made public, people might start asking questions about your relationship with Mr Harrison and exactly when it started. Perhaps it was convenient for you if Lord Hanley was out of the way. That's certainly what one could infer from these photos. Perhaps you should discuss this with Mr Harrison. If the press or police were to get hold of these photos, it would surely affect him, not to mention your little boy. The poor chap has been through so much already."

Lucy could feel her throat tightening and had to fight to control her voice. "One, I was defending myself in those photos. I have already spoken about being in an abusive relationship with Rupert and my medical records can back up my claims. Two, Rob is the last person in the world to be intimidated by you, and we both know we wouldn't be having this conversation if he was here with me right now. And three, if you ever threaten my son again, I will go to the press myself and make sure everyone from here to Westminster knows what a little creep you are."

With that she shoved him out of the way and marched down the corridor, using all her self-control not to break into a run.

IT WASN'T UNTIL later that evening, when Freddie was in bed and she and Rob were alone in the kitchen, that she told him what had happened.

"He threatened you?" asked Rob standing up, his face like thunder. Lucy put her hand on his arm to calm him.

"Not physically, but he had copies of some photos that Guy had taken on the night Rupert disappeared."

Lucy pushed them across the table towards him. Rob picked them both up and frowned.

"I don't understand."

"I lied about what happened that night. We argued. I thought he was going to hit me, so I picked up a spade and hit him first, then I ran home. Rachel was here. I told her what I'd done, and she went to check on him, but he'd gone."

Rob stared at her for a moment, his deep blue eyes blinking slowly as he took in everything she was telling him. Lucy waited nervously for him to speak, but when he didn't, she heard herself gabbling on again, trying to explain.

"I know I should have told the truth right from the start, but I was so scared they would lock me up. I know that's probably what I deserved, but I couldn't stand the thought of being away from Freddie. Then when they couldn't find him..." She trailed off before quietly adding, "You must think I'm a terrible coward."

Rob didn't respond, instead he asked, "Who else knows about this except, Rachel?"

"Meera and Jo," replied Lucy, beginning to chew her lip.

"And Jo didn't include it in any of her reports?"

"No. Maybe she should have done, but she wanted to help me." She couldn't stand this anymore. "Does this change things, between us, I mean?"

Rob's face broke into a smile. He reached over and stroked her hair. "Lucy, how could I ever think you are a coward? You are one of the bravest people I know, but I'm pleased you finally told me the truth. Now if I need to, I can help protect you too. I wish I could have done something when Rupert was alive. There were rumours that he'd started being violent but…"

He paused and his eyes settled on the photos on the table. Lucy followed his gaze. He reached over and picked them up. "What about these?" he asked.

"What do you think we should do?"

He moved over to the Aga and opened the lower door where several logs were smouldering away.

"I think the fewer copies in the world, the better. Agreed?"

"Agreed," replied Lucy quietly. Then she watched as he dropped the photos and they disappeared into the flames.

CHAPTER FOURTEEN

MEERA RAISED HER hand to shield her eyes from the low winter sun and watched nervously as the cherry picker rose higher into the air. Rob had sent two of his team to remove some of the ivy and wisteria from the walls of the Grange. Both plants had grown at such a rate over the summer that they were now in danger of reaching and damaging the roof. However, Meera had promised Krish she wouldn't do anything until they were sure there were no bats roosting there. After weeks of training his binoculars on the eaves, Krish had finally and a little sadly informed her that they were bat-free.

It had been over a week since Agnes had left. Life had returned to normal. Guy's court case was over with. The jury had found him guilty of all charges. As he had been declared unfit to stand trial, he couldn't be convicted, but it seemed unlikely that he would ever leave the psychiatric hospital where he had been receiving treatment since his arrest. When Meera had asked Lucy if she felt cheated in any way, her friend had merely shrugged and said she was happy to 'put the whole horrible business behind me'.

Meera had been as busy as ever at work. The colonel's health was slowly improving, Reverend Davenport wasn't getting any worse, but Caroline was still stubbornly refusing to discuss any sort of treatment. In a few weeks it would be Christmas and their wedding, but she still hadn't spoken to Ben about what she'd overheard his mother say. It had been on the tip of her tongue to say something when he returned from dropping Agnes off at the station, but he'd appeared in the kitchen and presented her with a huge bunch of her favourite white roses.

"Thank you for being so understanding about Mum. I know she isn't easy. To be honest, I was dreading her being here, but you were amazing."

"Thank you," Meera had said as she took the bouquet. He'd looked so happy and relieved, she couldn't bring herself to say anything else.

The cherry picker came to a halt above the first-floor windows and the young man in the basket set about pulling and chopping at the plants. Bits of twigs and leaves came tumbling to the ground. Meera took a step back and a sudden glint caught her eye.

"Have you found something?" she called up with her hands cupped around her mouth.

"There's a window hidden behind this lot. The frame looks sound, but the glass is a bit grubby. If you've got some soapy water, I'll give it a wash while I'm up here," the young man shouted back.

Meera hurried into the house, found a sponge and bucket in the utility and quickly filled it with detergent and warm water.

"What are you up to?" asked Ben as he returned from a visit to Dan Foxton's farm.

"Rob's men have found an attic window hidden beneath the ivy. They offered to clean it for me."

Ben stopped halfway through pulling his boots off and frowned. "They can't have done. Krish and I explored the attic a few weeks ago on one of his bat hunts. There were no windows. I remember saying it was a shame there was no natural light up there."

"Perhaps you didn't notice it because it was so over-grown," suggested Meera as she carefully carried the bucket to the door.

"Let me do that," offered Ben standing up and taking the bucket from her. "When I've seen which wall the window is on, I'll go up and have another look."

"Thank you," said Meera reaching up to remove a stray piece of straw from his hair before he disappeared through the door. Then she went into the kitchen to make some tea for the workmen.

After taking the tray of tea and biscuits outside, she returned to the kitchen, but there was still no sign of Ben, so she went to investigate herself. The attic of the Grange could be accessed by a narrow winding staircase behind a door in the corner of the landing.

"Ben! Are you up there?" she called out. There was a muffled noise in response that sounded like a 'yes'. Cautious-ly, Meera climbed the dusty stairs. Krish was fascinated by the attic, but she hadn't been up here since they first viewed the Grange with the estate agent.

"You are positive that there aren't any bats up here, aren't you?" she asked nervously.

"No, sadly. Krish and I were rather hoping to find a colony."

Ben's voice was clearer now, but she still couldn't see him.

"Where are you?" she called again.

"Here," replied Ben suddenly appearing at the far end of the attic. "What I thought was a solid wall is actually only a partition with a sliding panel."

Meera carefully made her way across the uneven, creaking floorboards to inspect what he'd found. Ben stepped to one side so she could peer through the opening. Inside it was only about six feet wide, but there was a pale shaft of light falling across the floor from the newly discovered and cleaned window. It was empty except for a large, old-fashioned steamer trunk.

The initials on the trunk, now tarnished with age, were J.B.T.

"I bet it's that archaeologist chap Sarah is studying. Joseph Baxter Tarrant. I read his name on the deeds."

Meera smiled at him affectionately. It was typical of him to have read through all the legal paperwork so thoroughly and to remember that sort of detail. He was one of the few people in the village who would happily listen to Sarah, who had a tendency to sound like she was giving a lecture whenever she discussed her favourite subject.

"Then I shall phone Rachel and let them know what we've found, in case they think it is important."

Meera wasn't left in any doubt how important her find was, when a breathless Sarah and Rachel arrived less than ten minutes after her call. Sarah's eyes were gleaming with almost religious devotion as she carefully picked up the notebook resting on top of the trunk.

"Do you think his notes will be helpful to your research?" she asked politely.

"Not only his notes and letters, Meera. The very fact that his name was on the deeds shows that he bought this place. He planned on staying here. He wasn't simply spending a few months in the village."

"Why wasn't that known? He must have left this place to someone. Couldn't you access his will?" asked Ben.

"There was so much secrecy around his death. His only living relative at the time was an elderly aunt. She was quite religious by all accounts and viewed suicide as a sin. After his death, she set up a scholarship in his name at his old college and the rest of his estate was put in a trust. It was quite a substantial amount and there was some confusion about where the money came from. It must have been the proceeds of the sale of the Grange."

Meera frowned. "I wonder why whoever cleared the house left his trunk up here."

Rachel looked up from the bundle of letters she had been reading. "These are love letters and it sounds to me like his lover was married. Maybe it was Joseph who hid his letters up here so nobody would find them or maybe he started packing and was planning on running away with her."

Meera leaned over her shoulder and began reading too. "The two of them sound so in love." She sighed. "Do you think he may have decided to take his own life, because she ended their relationship?"

"Would you mind if I took them back to the university with me?" asked Sarah, who was obviously more interested in his academic rather than his love life.

"Oh please do," said Meera, "as far as we're concerned they belong to you now, right?" She glanced over to Ben, who nodded his agreement. She was a little taken aback when Sarah immediately threw her arms around her and hugged her tight. They had all made an effort to be friendly to Rachel's girlfriend, but she'd always seemed rather distant.

"Thank you so much, both of you. Honestly, you don't know how important this could be to our research."

"You're very welcome," said Meera politely.

In truth she would be rather relieved to see the dusty old trunk go. Although the romantic in her had appreciated discovering the love letters, there were quite a few grubby marks on her new carpet where Ben had dragged it down from the attic and it was beginning to give the place a distinctly musty smell. She watched from the window as Rachel and Ben carried the trunk carefully to her car outside, while Sarah excitedly telephoned her team to share the news. No sooner had Meera waved Rachel and Sarah off, than another vehicle pulled up. It was Nish in one of the estate vans.

"What are you doing here?" she asked. "And why are you driving that?"

"I'm delivering the Christmas tree you ordered from the estate?"

"Oh, thank you. You seem to be fitting in well at the estate. Are you thinking of making a move here?" she asked as Nish went to the rear of the van and pulled out the netted six-foot tree.

"Nah, it's been good fun helping Lucy, but I'm really

only here for Becky."

"No offence taken," replied Meera sarcastically.

Nish grinned at her. "You and Krish too of course, but you know me—I'm more of a bright lights, big city kind of guy."

"Good. I think Mum and Dad would be upset if we both left them."

Nish rolled his eyes. "There are more big cities than Bradford you know, Meera. I'm not planning on staying there forever. And talking of parents. Have you spoken to Ben about his mother yet?"

"How do you know about that?"

"Mum told me. Remember we all agreed, after the whole Dev thing, no more secrets. You need to be honest with Ben." He gave her a meaningful look. "Get everything out in the open. I like being the cool uncle—don't leave it too late to make me one again."

Meera felt herself blush. She was about to tell her brother to mind his own business, but at that moment, Krish came charging out of the door.

"Uncle Nish, I didn't know you were here."

"Good timing, Krish mate. You can give me a hand."

Meera watched fondly as her son struggled under the weight of his end of the tree with a determined look on his face.

"Where do you want it, Mum?" he called over his shoulder.

"The drawing room, I think. Do you agree, Ben?" she called out, as she followed them in the house. Ben appeared from the kitchen where he'd been washing off the dust from the attic, but there was still a streak of dirt across his nose.

"Yes, sounds like a good idea. We could stand it in the bay window and sit round it to open our presents. The fireplace in there is perfect to hang stockings on."

They had already agreed that rather than go away on honeymoon, they would prefer to stay in Hartwell and spend their first Christmas together in their new home. Nish helped Ben put the tree in position and turned down Krish's offer to stay and help them decorate it.

"Sorry, mate. I've got more trees to drop off at the pub, school and church. I'll come and see it another day, okay?"

Then with a quick kiss goodbye for Meera, a high five for Krish and a slightly more awkward one for Ben, he headed back to his van.

"Can I go and get the box of decorations?" asked Krish excitedly. "I know where they are."

"Yes, of course," replied Meera.

"Would you like me to help you?" Ben called after him.

"No, I can manage," he shouted as he hurtled out of the room. Ben smiled as he wrapped his arm around Meera's shoulder and pulled her close.

"This Christmas is going to be great. I think I'm more excited than when I was a kid. And who knows, maybe one day there will be four stockings up there," said Ben inclining his head towards the carved wooden fireplace. "Wouldn't that be wonderful?"

"Yes, it really would," replied Meera quietly.

UNFORTUNATELY, MEERA HAD been to many funerals. She made a point of attending the final farewell of any of her patients. However, today's had to be the strangest. The ancient Celtic skeletons that had been found at the Hayloft were being returned to their graves. Rachel, who had thrown herself into learning about Druid culture over the last few months, had invited her friends to show their respects.

"After all," she'd said on more than one occasion, "it could well be our ancestors that we're laying to rest."

Although Meera was fairly confident she had no connection to the ancient bones that were about to be returned to the soil, she, Jo and Lucy still wanted to support their friend. They were joined by a handful of other villagers who were inquisitive or simply had nothing better to do. Sarah had also invited some local journalists in the hope of gaining some early publicity for the heritage centre, but they seemed far more interested in Lucy.

Meera usually enjoyed an opportunity to be part of her new community. Today, however, she was beginning to doubt her decision. There was an icy wind blowing and heavy drops of rain began to fall from the leaden sky. To make matters worse, it looked like it wouldn't be over with quickly. Sarah had tracked down a Druid priest to conduct a ceremony. Meera had been interested to see what she imagined would be a mystical figure; however, the small bald-headed man, wearing cords and a V-neck sweater, who had arrived in a dark brown hatchback, didn't look very inspiring. He had disappeared into the village hall to get changed and had appeared a few minutes later in white flowing robes. He carefully laid a circle of leaves around the grave and encouraged the mourners to form a circle too. Then he began the ceremony by calling for peace to the North, South, East and West.

As she observed this strange but quite moving ritual, Meera's thoughts drifted to her wedding. She'd had a productive morning, managing to book the string quartet she wanted, and had delivered her mother to Hartwell Hall. Her mother had insisted on helping Joan with the catering for the wedding. Although she appreciated her mother wanting to be involved, Meera had been a little anxious. She wasn't at all sure her mother would approve of Lucy's old-fashioned, chaotic kitchen or the three dogs who spent most of their time in there. Nor was she sure how Joan would take to having a stranger in her domain. On her way to the internment, she couldn't resist texting her mother to see how things were going. The response had been more positive than she could have hoped for.

Joan is lovely. We are getting on very well. The dogs are very smelly.

Finally, the internment ended and much to Sarah's obvious irritation the press surged forward to get a quote from Lucy. Meera turned away only to find herself face to face with Nora. The older woman seemed a little subdued and she couldn't quite look Meera in the eye.

"I'm sorry if what I said upset you the other day, Dr Kumar. I didn't mean any offence."

It sounded like she had been practising those two sentences many times and Meera was aware that they were being watched by the other villagers.

"Thank you for apologising, Mrs Parkin. Let's put the matter behind us, shall we?" she replied with a polite smile.

Nora gave a quick nod of her head and quickly scurried away.

"Now I've seen everything," murmured Jo who was standing next to her. "Maybe people have been boycotting the shop and her profits are hurting."

Lucy joined them, her coat collar turned up and her long blonde hair blowing in the wind.

"I heard Belinda, who was in the shop when it happened, had a quiet word and suggested a public apology might be in order."

"Good for Belinda," said Jo.

"She seems nice, doesn't she? Freddie said that the assembly she took at school was fun and her sermons are much shorter than the rev's. As fond as I am of him, I'm keeping my fingers crossed she's on duty for midnight mass." A sharp gust of wind blew in their faces, making them all gasp. "Why don't we head back home and sample whatever delicious things Joan and Meera's mum have been creating?" suggested Lucy.

"Good idea," replied Jo through chattering teeth.

"Are Rachel and Sarah going to join us?" asked Meera watching as the two of them tried to gain the interest of the journalist who was already heading back to his car.

"No, Sarah said they were busy when I asked them."

"That's a shame. I'd like to get to know Sarah better. We have invited them to dinner a couple of times, but Sarah always says she's busy with work."

Jo shook her head and tutted. "She must be mad to miss out on your cooking."

"Maybe she's shy. I know she's very clever and probably

gives amazing lectures, but you saw how she was at the village hall. Interacting isn't really her thing."

"Don't you ever get tired of seeing the best in people?" demanded Jo.

Lucy laughed good-naturedly. "Fortunately for you, no! I know I often get it wrong, but sometimes people can surprise you, like Nora just now. So generally, I give everyone the benefit of the doubt and hope they don't disappoint me."

At that moment, a Land Rover with a megaphone blaring out "Vote Devizes" drove by. The three of them watched the smug face of the leading candidate as he smiled and waved.

"I might make an exception for him," said Lucy.

Jo laughed, but Meera wondered if she should start following Lucy's example when it came to dealing with Agnes. After all, if Nora could be shown the error of her ways, anything could happen.

CHAPTER FIFTEEN

"I FEEL LIKE a princess," declared Lucy, twirling around. Meera's wedding was drawing ever closer, and they were at the final fitting for their bridesmaid dresses. Jo exchanged a glance with Rachel in the mirror they were both stood in front of. It was obvious from her expression that Rachel did not share Lucy's enthusiasm.

"It's all right for you," she grumbled. "You're tall. You look good in anything."

"Sorry, Meera. I think they are going to have to let my dress out. I can't breathe let alone move," gasped Jo, who was finding for the first time in her life she was putting on weight everywhere, not just her newly round stomach. Meera lifted her arm and peered at the seam of her dress.

"I think an inch on either side should do it. I'll let the seamstress know. Do you think the bonnets would be too much?"

"Meera, don't take this the wrong way, but if you make me wear a bonnet, I'll turn up in breeches and a frock coat like Ben and Jack," said Rachel.

Jo snorted and Meera looked crestfallen.

Lucy diplomatically stepped in. "Rach may have a point, Meera. The bonnets are quite large. I think the photographer might worry about our faces being hidden."

"Okay, you might be right," she agreed, "but I so want everything to be perfect. For a while everything seemed to be going wrong. Not being able to find a venue, then Ben's mother not being what I expected. I thought it was the universe's way of telling me I was going too fast."

Lucy wrapped her arm around Meera's shoulder. "You are allowed to have a wobble. You've moved house and got divorced, two of the most stressful things we can go through in life."

"When did you get so wise?" asked Rachel.

"I've always been wise," retorted Lucy flicking her hair back, then she grinned. "I just hid it well. Actually, I had a bit of a wobble recently and Rob helped me see I was getting things out of proportion."

"What was your wobble about?" asked Jo.

"The Hartwell curse. When Sarah talked about it at the village hall, I started panicking and thinking about taking Freddie away from here. I thought me doing well in the polls was a sign we should move to London."

"You aren't going to, are you? Krish would miss him terribly," said Meera.

"No. I was only being silly. Freddie would hate to leave Hartwell."

"Good. We'd miss you too and goodness knows how Bill and Joan would cope."

"Oh, speaking of Joan," said Lucy, "it's her sixtieth birthday next week. She's adamant she doesn't want a fuss, but I can't not celebrate it. Bill is taking her out for lunch at their favourite restaurant, then I thought I'd do a girls' afternoon tea for her and her friends. I'd love it if you could come as well—and don't worry, I won't attempt to bake. I've already ordered the cake."

At that moment, Lucy's phone rang. She looked at the screen. "It's Alison from the Rosemary Centre. Do you mind if I take it?" she asked and hurried over to the far corner of the room.

Meera produced a tape measure and turned her attention back to Jo's dress. "I wonder if different underwear would help?" she mused.

Jo rolled her eyes at Rachel. "I'm already wearing massive granny knickers and I've gone up a bra size."

Suddenly Lucy let out a squeal of excitement and punched the air. "That's fantastic news! Thank you so much for telling me. Let's get together soon and celebrate!"

"Well?" asked Jo, who like the other two had been watching in bemused silence, when she finally put the phone down.

"They've got the money," said Lucy breathlessly.

"From central government?" asked Rachel.

"No. It came from an anonymous donor. Their accountant got a call this morning from a merchant bank in London. They had instructions from their client to make a transfer into the Rosemary Centre account. They'll still need to keep fundraising, but there is enough to allow them to move to Moorhead Farm and operate from there for at least the next five years." She paused to catch her breath as Meera and Rachel both began congratulating her.

"What does this mean for your election campaign?" asked Jo, whose suspicious mind had just gone up a gear.

Lucy frowned and shrugged her shoulders. "I guess I withdraw. All I ever wanted to do was secure the future of the Rosemary Centre."

"Really?" asked Rachel. "Because it looks like you could win, you know."

"Yes, and for a little while I thought that was what I wanted, when I was having my wobble, but even after everything that's happened here, I don't want to leave Hartwell. So, I'll be one of those rare politicians who keeps their word. What's with the frown, Jo?"

"Devizes is from a family of merchant bankers," replied Jo. "You are inching ahead of him in the polls. Could it really only be a coincidence?"

"Actually, there was a rather unpleasant incident with him on the day I gave evidence. He had the copies of the photos you found in Guy's safe."

"Why didn't you tell me?" demanded Jo.

"I guess I got distracted with the verdict and everything else. Besides nothing came of it. He was only making empty threats."

"What photos?" asked Rachel.

"They show me arguing with Rupert on the night he disappeared. I'm holding the spade," explained Lucy.

"Oh my God, Lucy!"

"It's fine. Jo found them months ago and nothing has happened. Guy's trial is over; the investigation into Rupert's death is closed."

"Are you sure? Because Sarah said there was some guy hanging around the Hayloft. He was asking questions at the dig the other day."

Jo's ears pricked up. "Did he have a London accent? Driving a BMW?"

"Sarah didn't mention a car, but yes, she said he was from down south."

"It's DS Simon Spencer. He's up here trying to find a connection between two armed robbers he arrested and Rupert. And before you ask, I didn't mention it because I didn't want to worry you and I don't think there is a connection other than they used Rupert's shotguns."

"How did they get those? Did he sell them for drugs?" asked Lucy.

"No, Caroline sent them to an auction house and they were stolen from there. Sorry, I thought she might have told you by now."

"Caroline never tells me anything. Oh well, as she and Alexander bought them, I suppose they were hers to sell."

"Other bridesmaids talk about flower arrangements and seating plans when they're trying on their dresses. Mine talk about guns and armed robbers," grumbled Meera as she unzipped a relieved Jo.

"Sorry, Meera," apologised Lucy.

"At least you can't accuse us of being boring," replied Rachel. "Let's just hope none of us are arrested before the big day."

As Jo drove to Northallerton, later that afternoon, she thought about Devizes and what Lucy had told her. The whole thing made her feel very uneasy. Only a few days ago, she'd seen him sitting with Simon Spencer in one of the pubs in Northallerton. She'd thought it was strange at the time. Apart from both living in London, she couldn't imagine what the two men would have in common, but she had managed to find out why Spencer was so keen to get involved in the Hanley case. She'd made a few phones calls to old colleagues, who confirmed what she suspected. Wallace was due to return to her position as head of the team, replacing Palmer. Spencer had never seen eye to eye with Wallace and wanted to impress her with a murder conviction, so she wouldn't try to shift him to vice along with Palmer.

Jo had been back at work for over a week. As Meera and everyone else had promised, now she was a little further into her pregnancy, she felt she had new lease of life. However, after her fainting episode she was still desk-bound while Spencer swanned around the place. Dawson had been assigned to assist him. Most of the time Dawson drove her mad. Since he'd found out she was pregnant he kept bringing her cups of milky tea and chocolate biscuits and despite her complaints, he'd insisted on decorating her desk with tinsel and a white plastic Christmas tree. However, seeing him willingly trot after Spencer and listen open-mouthed to all his tall tales had stung. She didn't know where they had disappeared off to now, but Spencer had left her a note.

Can you check witness statements taken during Hanley investigation? See if anyone mentions seeing someone matching my guys' description.

"I'm not your bloody secretary," she muttered as she

went to retrieve the file. "Not even a please or thank you."

As nobody else was in the office, she flicked on the radio. It was already tuned to the local station. Lucy had arranged to announce that she intended to stand down during the lunchtime news bulletin. Jo listened as her friend explained that she had achieved her goal and the future of the Rosemary Centre was now secure.

"May I ask, which candidate you will now be lending your support to?" asked the interviewer.

"Heather Rhodes," replied Lucy immediately. "She's by far the best candidate. She understands the needs of the constituency and has some amazing ideas. Besides, the other three are absolutely ghastly."

Jo grinned and shook her head. It was Lucy's refreshingly open and honest answers that had made her so popular.

As she could have told Spencer, nobody had said they'd seen anyone from outside the village around the time Rupert disappeared. Not even Nora. It was during the first lockdown and people barely left their homes. Her eyes were beginning to glaze over when the chief constable paid her an impromptu visit. When he saw what she was doing, he shook his head.

"I know Spencer thinks he's on to something, but I can't help thinking it could turn into a wild goose chase," he said as he glanced through the file on Rupert's disappearance.

"With Inspector Wallace coming back from maternity leave, I think he wants to impress her," replied Jo.

"Ah ha, I thought as much. Office politics, eh?" he commented with a shake of his head as he left quietly humming a Christmas carol to himself.

After a boring, fruitless afternoon, she was relieved to turn off her computer at five o'clock and drive back to Hartwell. Every house and cottage seemed to have a Christmas tree in the window and a wreath on the door. Her cottage was the same. Jack had bought a massive tree that practically filled the whole sitting room. Mistletoe hung in every doorway and there was barely a surface that hadn't been draped in tinsel.

She parked her car and walked up to the White Hart to meet Jack, thinking how lucky she was to have ended up with a man like him instead of a Devizes or a Spencer. He was honest, loyal and kind, everything they weren't, and he was going to be an amazing dad. Their daughter was going to have a wonderful childhood, full of fun and laughter, with birthday parties, visits from Father Christmas, holidays to the seaside—all the things Jo had missed out on.

Wham's 'Last Christmas' was playing loudly when she arrived at the pub, but unusually there weren't many customers.

"Evening, lovely!" Jack greeted her with a huge smile and leaned over the bar to kiss her beneath yet another sprig of mistletoe. "How was your day?"

"Between being too fat for my bridesmaid dress and spending the afternoon reading witness statements, I'd kill for a chilled beer, but as that's not allowed…"

"A glass of our finest mineral water coming up."

"Where is everyone?" she asked as she hoisted herself on to one of the bar stools.

"It's the school carol concert at the church—half the village will be there. I hope the pastry on those pies is up to standard, Mother!" he teased, as his mother made her way back to the kitchen after delivering two plates of food to some customers sitting by the log fire.

"May I suggest in the future you use chilled butter, dear," Shirley repeated in a perfect imitation of Agnes. "What a cheek! People come from miles around for my pies. Who did she think she was?"

Shirley stomped out of the bar with her hands on her hips.

"Oh dear," said Jack with a grin as the kitchen door slammed behind his mother. "She doesn't take well to criticism. It'll be a long time before she forgets that."

"You shouldn't keep reminding her. She got Agnes spot on though," replied Jo. "The accent was perfect."

"Yep, Mum's always been a good mimic and she can do loads of accents. She trained to be an actress down in London."

"I didn't know she'd studied there. What happened?"

"Nothing really came of it. She got a few auditions. She even made it into the chorus for a season of *Anything Goes* in the West End, then she met Dad. He swept her off her feet and they landed back in Hartwell."

Jo shifted in her seat. She'd seen photos of Charlie, Jack's dad, a big bear of a man, who looked like his son, but neither Jack nor Shirley mentioned him very often.

"How come you don't talk about your dad much?" she asked.

Jack shrugged. "I think it upsets Mum. Sometimes when she's had a few too many vodkas, she'll start talking about him, but she always gets a bit teary."

"I know he had a heart attack, but how long ago was it?"

"I was nineteen. I'd just represented England for the first time at Twickenham. He and Mum were watching me. I'd scored the winning try. They were both on their feet cheering. He hugged Mum, said, 'Can you believe that's our boy out there?' then he collapsed. And that was it. There were loads of medics around. They tried to save him, but it was no good."

His face didn't show much emotion, but Jo could hear his voice catch on the last word. She reached over and stroked his arm.

"I'm so sorry," she said softly.

"At least he got to see me play." He turned away to pull himself a pint and then raised his glass to the photo of his father that was positioned between the optics of his two favourite whiskies. "Cheers, Dad!"

"Cheers, Charlie," echoed Jo.

Jack put his glass down. "I was thinking, and say if you hate the idea, but I wondered if we could call the baby Charlotte, maybe just as a middle name. I thought it might be nice, but like I said if you hate it…"

Jo leaned across and kissed him.

"I love it. We'll call her Charlotte. Charlie for short."

CHAPTER SIXTEEN

RACHEL SLOWLY OPENED her eyes and stretched. School had finished for Christmas, and she was a lady of leisure for the next two and a half weeks. As her leg came into contact with cold cotton, she realised she was alone. Sitting up with a jolt, she looked over to the other side of the bed. It was obvious it hadn't been slept in. Reaching for her dressing gown, she pulled it on and hurried downstairs. She found Sarah where she'd left her the previous evening, sitting in front of her computer screen at their small dining table surrounded by the papers and notes from Meera's attic.

"Have you been down here all night?" she asked yawning widely. "I swear you haven't slept since Ben and Meera gave us that trunk."

"I know, but it's been worth it. Joseph's notes are absolutely fascinating. Do you remember I said we were struggling to make sense of the inscription on the Hartwell nobles?" Rachel nodded as she yawned again. "According to Joseph there was a similar inscription around the old well, but I can't recall ever seeing anything."

"I'm not surprised. It's been covered with moss for as long as I can remember. There's always been an argument between the parish council and the Hartwell estate as to whose responsibility it is to maintain it."

"Well, hopefully when you join the council, you'll be able to do something about it. I'm going to head down there and take a look."

"Now? Don't you want some breakfast first or a cup of tea at least?"

"No thanks. I've been drinking coffee all night. I'm buzzing."

"Okay. I'm going to grab a shower then call in and see Mum. I want to ask her if she needs a lift up to Joan's birthday party tomorrow. You haven't forgotten, have you?"

"No, I'll be there," replied Sarah as she headed out the door.

RACHEL WALKED INTO the farmhouse kitchen. Becky was sitting by the Aga, flicking through a magazine.

"Where's Mum?" she asked.

Becky didn't bother looking up. "She's taken Minty to York to get some new pyjamas, then have a pizza and look at the Christmas lights."

"Why didn't you go with them?"

"They like spending time together and besides I've got a shift at the pub in half an hour," her sister said defensively.

Rachel sighed. Since moving back into the farmhouse, it felt like Becky had reverted to being a child again. She let Mary do all the cooking and cleaning for her and Minty. There was a huge pile of dirty dishes in the sink. Rachel turned on the taps and tossed a tea towel to her sister.

"I'll wash. You dry."

Pouting and flicking her hair, Becky joined her at the large Belfast sink. As she reached over for the first soapy plate, Rachel noticed a pretty silver charm bracelet dangling from her wrist.

"A present from Nish?" she asked.

"No. Don't be nosy."

"I was only asking. No need to bite my head off. I thought the two of you were spending a lot of time together that's all. I hadn't seen it before, and I thought you'd sold all your jewellery to pay Mum back."

"I did. Even my wedding ring. If you must know, Miss Marple, the bracelet is a present from Colonel Marsden. It belonged to his late wife."

"Why did he give it to you?"

"Why wouldn't he?" Becky shot back. "I've been helping him while he gets back on his feet again."

"He's a kind man. I hope you aren't taking advantage of him."

Becky stopped what she was doing and glared at her. "How dare you! He gave Meera his Hartwell noble too, but I don't see you pointing the finger at her. In fact, he gave a watch to Shirley, a necklace to Joan and a ring each to Mum and Caroline. He said he wanted the pleasure of giving Annabel's jewellery away rather than bequeath it in his will. It was a lovely thing to do, but you have to spoil it by practically accusing me of stealing from him."

With that Becky threw the mug she was holding back in the sink, showering Rachel in dishwater. Rachel opened her mouth to protest, but her sister had already gone. Wiping the soapsuds from her face, she finished the washing up alone.

As Rachel stomped out of the farmhouse, she almost bumped into Meera leaving the dower house.

"Oh my goodness! What's wrong? You've got a face like thunder."

"Becky! She drives me mad. I hope Nish knows what he is letting himself in for. I asked her a perfectly reasonable question about the bracelet the colonel gave her, and she bit my head off. I only wanted to check that he had meant to give it to her."

Meera gave her a sympathetic smile. "On this occasion, I really think you should have believed Becky. The colonel has been giving away a lot of his late wife's things. Divvying up he called it. I actually think he found it quite therapeutic. I really think you should give Becky the benefit of the doubt. I have decided that's what I'm going to do with Agnes."

Rachel looked at her incredulously. "Even after what you heard her say?"

"Yes, after all she didn't say it to me directly."

"Your mother seemed to have a pretty clear idea of what she meant."

Rachel had spoken to Meera's mum when she last visited, and she was still fuming about the incident.

"Well, she wasn't there either," replied Meera sounding defensive. "She and Dad had a much harder time than me and Nish when we first came over. They have always tried to protect us." She paused. "I know you and Jo always say Lucy is a terrible judge of character, but I've begun to admire the way she sees the best in people. Inevitably sometimes she's let down, but I've decided I'm going to be more like Lucy."

Rachel was slightly sceptical of this theory. She'd known Meera since they were both students and this sounded like her typically sticking her head in the sand to avoid confrontation. However, after arguing with Becky she didn't want to fall out with Meera too so all she said was: "I'll remind you of this conversation if things between Nish and Becky get serious. You could end up with her as a sister-in-law."

"Oh dear," replied Meera with a frown. "My parents are only just getting used to the idea of me remarrying." Then her face brightened. "On the plus side you and I would be related."

Rachel laughed and gave her friend a hug. "I'm liking this new worry-free Meera."

Rachel left her old friend, still smiling at her new-found optimism.

THE FOLLOWING DAY, Rachel was getting ready for Joan's birthday party. She checked her watch. They were due at Hartwell Hall soon, but Sarah still wasn't back from working down at the well. Yesterday, she had successfully scraped off some moss and discovered the hidden inscription, and today she and her team were investigating further. Rachel had barely heard from her all day except for a text half an hour ago that simply said:

Sorry, Rachel. I'm running late but heading home now. See you soon x

Rachel loved the way Sarah always used proper grammar and spelling in her text messages—and that she thought of the cottage as home. She surveyed her reflection critically in the bedroom mirror. She was wearing a new purple velvet shift dress. black opaque tights and ankle boots with a block heel to give her a bit of extra height. She had bought the dress a couple of months ago in York. Meera had told her the A-line design was flattering, but if she breathed out you could still see her stomach. Thank God she'd been running every day, or she probably wouldn't have fit into it. She heard the door slam downstairs and Sarah called out her name. Rachel grabbed her jacket and hurried downstairs.

"Sorry, I'm late," said Sarah rushing in. "I'll jump in the shower and change. I promise it won't take more than ten minutes." She looked flustered. Her cheeks were flushed and most of her curls had escaped from her scrunchie. She placed a quick kiss on Rachel's cheek before shrugging off her coat.

"I was getting worried. Is everything okay?" asked Rachel.

"Yes, fine, but it's been quite an afternoon," explained Sarah sitting down to pull off her boots. "Firstly, that detective from London turned up when we were finishing off at the Hayloft. Remember I said he was hanging around the other day?"

Rachel made a face. She had only met Simon briefly, but she had not been impressed. Talk about thinking he was God's gift. She'd no idea what Jo had ever seen in him.

"He started going on about what a coincidence it was that we were digging in the same place that Rupert was last seen."

Rachel felt a shiver run through her, but she didn't say a word.

"He asked if we'd ever dug up something that could have been used to hit him with. He said he'd spoken to a mate of his in forensics who thought something smooth and flat could have caused the injury to Rupert's skull," continued Sarah. "Anyway I told him we had but they were all almost two thousand years old and that we had moved on from that area and were now concentrating on the well. I thought that would be the end of it, but then something weird happened." She paused, obviously expecting some sort of reaction, but Rachel just stared at her blankly, not trusting herself to speak, so Sarah carried on, "One of our students, who was scraping away the moss, dropped a chisel down the well and we all heard it hit something metal. So we sent a camera down there and saw a spade had got wedged halfway down. We managed to get it out. It was clearly quite modern and what's more there was a reddish-brown stain on it. I immediately remembered what Spencer had said and called him. He and that chubby officer turned up and they seemed pretty excited."

"Oh my God, Sarah! What have you done?" whispered Rachel. She went over to the window and gripped on to the sill to steady herself. Outside the village was in darkness except for the fairy lights outside the White Hart and the lamp above the church gates. Her mind was racing, but before she could gather her thoughts, a BMW pulled up outside the pub. Her pounding heart almost stopped.

"What's wrong?" asked Sarah. Rachel didn't reply as she

watched Spencer and Dawson step out of the car and stride purposefully towards the pub. Without saying a word, Rachel dashed to the door and ran across the street to the Hart. She arrived, slightly out of breath, to find Jo, Jack and Rob sitting around the table by the fire. Laying in front of them on the table was the spade in a plastic evidence bag. On the handle it was still possible to see some of the plastic label: RHP, Robert Harrison Properties. DS Spencer, the detective from London was speaking.

"Can you confirm this spade is your property, Mr Harrison?"

"It is," said Rob quietly, his face impassive.

"Robert Harrison, I am arresting you on suspicion of the murder of Lord Rupert Hanley. You do not have to say anything…"

"This is crazy," protested Jack. "Rob was in here the night Rupert disappeared. He was playing snooker with me and Dan until midnight."

Rob stood up and patted Jack on the shoulder. "It's okay, Jack," he said, "but do me a favour and let Lucy know what's happened." He paused and looked directly at Jo. "Tell her not to say anything. I'm okay with this. Jo, make sure she knows that?"

Jo nodded dumbly. Dawson clapped a pair of handcuffs on him and he seemed to notice Rachel for the first time. He gave her a half-smile.

"Don't worry, Rach. I'll be fine." She opened her mouth to protest, but he shook his head firmly at her. "No heroics, okay? You need to stay strong for Lucy."

She watched helplessly as Rob was led to the waiting police car. Jack turned to Jo.

"What's going on?" he asked. "Rob didn't kill Rupert. Why didn't you say anything?"

Jo stood up and grabbed her coat. "It's a really long story, Jack. I promise I'll explain later. Come on, Rachel, it looks like we'll have to spoil Joan's birthday party."

Chapter Seventeen

J OAN'S BIRTHDAY PARTY was in full swing when Rachel and Jo arrived. Joan, Mary, Shirley and Caroline were all sitting around the fire, admiring the Christmas tree and eating mince pies, while Lucy kept topping up their cups with tea.

"Finally, you're here! We thought you'd got lost," she said, then paused, taking in their serious expressions. "Has something happened?"

"Rob's been arrested for Rupert's murder," said Jo, bluntly.

Lucy stepped back as though she'd been punched. "What? Why?"

"They found the spade I threw down the well," said Rachel.

The room had gone very quiet, but there were no gasps or exclamations of surprise. Lucy felt as if all the air had been sucked out of her. She sank down on to the arm of one of the sofas. Her mind was a whirl.

"Perhaps you should telephone Harrowell," suggested Caroline instead, calmly placing her teacup back on its saucer.

"I don't think he wants you to. I don't think he has any

intention of defending himself. He told us to tell you he's okay with this," said Rachel, quietly.

Lucy felt her heart racing. She turned to Jo, who was looking unusually worried and had flopped down on the sofa next to Joan.

"Can't you do something, Jo? Tell them they've got it wrong."

"Of course I could," she almost snapped. "As soon as Dawson and Spencer appeared looking so smug with that stupid spade—but like Rachel said, Rob didn't want me too. I think he's prepared to go down for it."

"You all seem convinced he's innocent," said Caroline still as composed as ever. Lucy's mind suddenly stopped racing. She knew exactly what she needed to do. She was going to have to confess everything that happened that night. There was no way she could let Rob go to prison for her and he would—she was sure of that. Rachel and Jo were right, he would admit to killing Rupert to protect her. She took a deep breath and turned to her mother-in-law.

"I'm so sorry, Caroline. I haven't been honest with you. Rupert and I argued on the night he disappeared, and I hit him with a spade…"

Caroline held up her hand to interrupt her. "I know. He told me."

"What? When?" stammered Lucy.

"That evening. He arrived at my door, blood dripping down his face and ranting like a madman. He demanded I hand over his father's guns. He kept saying he wanted to teach you a lesson."

Lucy's hand flew to her mouth. "Oh my God! He wanted to shoot me."

"I believed so, yes. I tried to calm him down. My first idea was to put some sedatives in his whisky. I only had a small amount, enough to make him drowsy, but he knocked it back and threw the glass against the wall. Then he barged his way into the study. He knew the code for the gun cabinet. He wouldn't stop ranting. I really did think he would kill you and probably me, if I tried to stop him. I simply couldn't let him get hold of the guns. I was pleading with him, pulling his arms, begging him to calm down, but he pushed me away and started threatening me." She paused. The room was deadly silent. Caroline looked Lucy directly in the eye. "I picked up the marble paperweight from the desk and I hit him. He fell to the floor and that was it."

To Lucy it felt as if time was standing still. "It was you who killed him. I don't believe it," she whispered, although even as she spoke the words, she knew Caroline was telling her the truth.

"I had to stop him. It was history repeating itself. My son was going to become a murderer just like his father."

Lucy looked at her guests. Rachel and Jo appeared to be as shocked as she felt, but the three older ladies were amazingly composed.

"Wait! Who did Alexander kill?" asked Rachel.

"Joseph. His name was Joseph Tarrant Baxter."

"The archaeologist buried in the churchyard? He committed suicide. Sarah knows all about it."

"No, he didn't. Alexander shot him and made it look like suicide. I couldn't stop him and like a coward I remained silent, but I wasn't going to stand by and let a Hanley take another innocent life."

"Why did Alexander shoot Joseph?" asked Lucy.

"Because I was in love with him and was going to leave Alexander to be with him."

Lucy felt her brain needed to speed up to understand everything she was being told. She was still trying to process the fact Caroline may well have saved her life.

"What did you do next?" she asked.

"Yes, how did he end up in the cave?" added Rachel.

Caroline took a sip of her tea and Mary gave a small cough. She glanced around the room before turning to her daughter.

"We helped Caroline. When she told us what she'd done, Shirley, Joan and I went to the dower house."

"You moved a dead body? Rupert's body? I don't believe it," said Rachel, shaking her head incredulously.

"We had to help her. She's one of our oldest friends and she needed us, love," said Shirley softly, reaching out to pat Caroline on her shoulder. Caroline gave her a weak smile.

"They helped me just as they had once before, when I found out I was pregnant with Joseph's baby."

"Rupert wasn't Alexander's?" asked Lucy.

"No, of course he was, Lucinda," tutted Caroline, for a second looking more like herself again. "Rupert was almost identical to Alexander, in all ways sadly. When I discovered I was pregnant by Joseph, I planned to leave Alexander, but he must have realised something was going on before I could speak to him." She took a deep breath. "He was working for the foreign and commonwealth office at the time. After killing Joseph, he was posted overseas for six months. I hid myself away here with Rupert, but when the time came, I went down to London."

"What happened to the baby?" asked Jo, who had remained silent, but whose eyes hadn't left Caroline's face.

"I think you probably already know," said Caroline, returning her gaze.

It was Joan who gently laid her hand on Jo's arm. "Mary and I went down to London with Caroline, and Shirley stayed up here at the Hall with Jack and Rupert in case Alexander telephoned," she began to explain. "You know how good she is a mimicking people. She could do an excellent impersonation of Caroline—still can."

"It wasn't difficult. The line from the Caribbean wasn't great in those days and a conversation with Alexander rarely lasted longer than five minutes," added Shirley.

"The three of us went to stay with Annabel Marsden," continued Joan. "She had a flat in the tower and Hugh was away on manoeuvres with his old regiment at the time. He had no idea what was going on. When the time came Mary and I delivered the baby."

"How did I end up outside Great Ormond Street?"

"I left you there with a note asking you to be called Jo after your father," said Joan quietly. "I'd worked there as a student nurse and knew the entrances the staff were most likely to use."

"And the Hartwell noble?" said Jo quietly. Her face was impossible to read.

Joan nodded. "Yes," she said, "perhaps it was silly and sentimental of me, but I knew by then Bill and me would never have any children of our own to leave it to. For a little while, I wondered if we could adopt you and maybe raise you as our own, but Caroline was terrified Alexander would find out. He really wasn't a very nice man. Still, I wanted you to have something, to show that we did care about you." Joan wiped a tear away from her eye. "I think part of me even believed it might help keep you safe. I waited in the phone box across the road. I was going to make an anonymous call to the hospital, but I didn't need to. Only a few minutes after I left you two nurses came outside and found you and took you inside."

Lucy's gaze flicked anxiously between Jo and Caroline, but both women had their eyes fixed on the floor and wore the same inscrutable expressions. She couldn't imagine what they both must be thinking. It was so terribly sad. Jo growing up without a family and how on earth did Caroline cope with giving away her baby? She gave her head a shake. Right now, she needed to focus on Rob.

"I can't let Rob take responsibility for killing Rupert," she said quietly.

Caroline looked up finally and cleared her throat. "He won't have to, Lucinda. I'll do what I should have done a long time ago. I'll go to the police."

"No, Caroline!" protested Mary, who looked close to tears. "It's bad enough you won't accept any treatment because you think you don't deserve to live."

"She's ill," explained Shirley. "If they send her to prison, she could die there. It isn't fair. She's been through such a lot."

"But this isn't only about Caroline. The police won't believe she could move a body without any help. They'll start asking questions. What about the other three? They could get into trouble too. They could be charged with, I don't know, assisting an offender, concealing a body. My mum can't go to prison," said Rachel a note of panic in her voice.

"She might not have to," said Jo. Everyone turned to look at her. "There might be a way that we can get Rob released without anyone here getting into trouble. Jack said Rob was in the pub with him that night. Can you confirm that too, Shirley?"

"Yes, definitely," replied Shirley looking more serious than Lucy had ever seen her. "It was the night the first lockdown was announced. The place was heaving. Jack was worried about what would happen to the business and Rob was trying to cheer him up. They had a lock-in after closing and played snooker. When I came back from helping Caroline, they were both fast asleep in the games room. I locked the door and went to bed."

"Good, but if anyone asks, don't mention the bit about helping Caroline," ordered Jo. "Lucy have you still got those photographs I found in Guy's safe?"

"No. I burnt them."

Jo looked at her in astonishment. "What the hell did you do that for?"

"Because Devizes had a copy of them and was threatening to give them to the police or press. When I told Rob, we thought the fewer copies the better. Have I messed up?"

"Not necessarily. Are you positive the photos were the same? Did they have the time and date on like the ones you had?"

Lucy screwed up her face as she tried to recall that day in

the courthouse. "Yes, definitely. In the bottom right-hand corner, just like mine did."

"Good! And actually that might explain what those two were doing together." Jo seemed to be almost talking to herself, then she stood up suddenly and pointed at Lucy and Caroline.

"I want you two to come to the station with me in case this doesn't work out. Shirley, you and Jack phone the station and tell them Rob was in the pub all night. See if you can get anyone else who was there that night and saw him to ring too. Try to create a bit of a fuss."

LUCY CLIMBED INTO the passenger seat of Jo's car while Caroline sat in the back.

"Don't you think the two of you should talk about, you know, everything?" ventured Lucy as they sped away from the hall in silence.

"No," snapped Jo, "I've got more important things to think about right now. I need to have what we say to Spencer clear in my head. Let me concentrate and I'll tell you what I want you to say."

Lucy managed to remain silent for ten whole minutes. She could feel the panic rising inside her as she thought about Rob languishing in a cell, prepared to go to prison to protect her. Her eyes flicked anxiously between Jo's determined face and Caroline's shell-shocked expression staring back at her in the rear-view mirror. Finally, she couldn't stand the tension any longer.

"So what's the plan, Jo?" she asked tentatively, fully expecting to have her head bitten off.

Instead, Jo took a deep breath and began to explain. "Spencer is going to try to say you killed or at least knocked out Rupert with the spade and that Rob either finished him off or moved his body. He's probably going to make out that the two of you were already in a relationship."

"But we weren't!" protested Lucy, but Jo ignored her.

"Listen to me, it is very important that we deny knowing the photos exist and that when they show them to you, you say you took a swing at Rupert with the spade in self-defence but did not make contact and he stumbled and fell. Have you got that?"

"Yes," replied Lucy obediently, feeling more nervous than ever.

"If they ask you why you never mentioned the spade in your statement, you'll have to say you were confused or too upset at the time and forgot. In this instance, you being a dizzy blonde might actually work to our advantage. But remember, if anyone asks you a question say the bare minimum, like when you were in court. Don't start twittering on. We need them to believe that Rupert was alive when you left him, that it was not you, but Guy who was the last person to see him alive. Those damn photos show he was there and his obsession with you gives him a strong motive. That combined with Shirley backing up Rob's alibi should be enough to get him released."

"And if it isn't?" asked Lucy quietly.

"Then we'll have to tell the truth. Agreed?"

"Agreed," replied Lucy.

Jo raised her eyes to the rear-view mirror, looking at her back-seat passenger for the first time.

"Agreed," replied Caroline so softly that Lucy could barely hear her.

They arrived at the police station and Lucy and Caroline almost had to run to keep up with Jo as she marched up to the office where Dawson and Spencer were sitting. They both looked startled as the three of them barged in without knocking.

"What are you playing at?" Jo demanded. "Rob Harrison was questioned when Rupert disappeared. He's got an alibi. He was in the pub all night."

"It was his best mate who gave him that alibi. He wouldn't be the first person to lie for a friend. You know that, even if you are sleeping with him," replied Spencer.

"That's irrelevant," snapped Jo.

Spencer shrugged. "When he was questioned last time, he didn't have a motive. Now he's living with Hanley's widow, and we only have their word for when that relationship started."

Lucy felt herself flush. She hated the way he spoke as if she wasn't there, but Jo had told her very firmly not to say anything unless she was directly asked a question.

"What's more," continued Spencer, "we now have a possible weapon that belongs to him. He's got a previous conviction for assault and, most importantly, he hasn't denied it. He hasn't even asked for a solicitor."

"Why did you suddenly become interested in Rob? You've been hanging around the Hayloft for a few days," asked Jo, her tone a little less challenging.

"A hunch. All good coppers act on them or have you forgotten that?" asked Spencer sarcastically.

Before Jo could respond, Dawson reached under his desk and handed her a folder. "Devizes gave him these."

Spencer's smug grin had disappeared, but Jo gave Dawson a grateful smile as she opened the folder and pulled out the photos Devizes had shown Lucy.

"He got them from Guy Lovell's safe. You remember, you said you thought someone had been there before when we searched his place," said Dawson. Spencer was scowling now, and Lucy thought he might actually thump Dawson.

Jo raised an eyebrow. "Do you think that falls under assisting an offender or tampering with evidence?"

"You tell me," Spencer snapped back. "According to Devizes you gave copies of these photos to your friend here." He pointed at Lucy, but kept his eyes fixed on Jo, who had a look of surprise on her face.

"I've never seen these photos before in my life. You are welcome to search my cottage and Hartwell Hall if you don't believe me."

At that moment, the chief constable arrived in the doorway. Jo, Spencer and Dawson all sprang to their feet.

"Good afternoon, Lady Hanley," the chief constable said addressing Caroline, then nodding to Lucy, "Lady Hanley," before turning to his officers. "Can one of you tell me what is going on? The switchboard is practically jammed with phone calls from residents of Hartwell."

"Spencer has arrested Rob Harrison in connection with the Rupert Hanley case, but he has an alibi."

"I thought you were here to find a connection to the two

London gangsters who used Hanley's guns in a robbery," said the chief constable.

"I was, sir, but I've been working on a theory," said Spencer switching his charming smile back on. "Recently, some photographs came into my possession. They show Lucy Hanley arguing with her husband the night he disappeared and brandishing a spade. There is no way his wife could have moved Hanley's body on her own. I think Harrison helped her. The spade belonged to him and the two of them are now in a relationship."

"It's all just speculation," argued Jo.

"What about the spade we found hidden down the well? I bet it's the same one she's holding in those photos. The right expert would be able to confirm that, and I think it could tie in with the fracture to Hanley's skull."

"Anyone could have thrown it down the well. We don't even know how long it has been there. I take it forensics didn't find anything incriminating, like blood?" argued Jo.

"No, nothing. That mark was only rust," confirmed Dawson.

The chief constable was now studying the photos. "Where did these come from?"

"Seb Devizes gave them to me," said Spencer.

"He took them from Guy Lovell's safe, before we had a chance to search the place," added Jo.

"I see," replied the chief constable. He looked up and fixed his eyes on Lucy. "Lady Hanley, when you reported your husband missing, I recall you mentioning an argument, but not that you hit him with a spade."

"I'm terribly sorry," stammered Lucy as her cheeks burnt

under the gaze of four police officers. "I must have forgotten. It was such a muddling time, and Rupert and I did argue rather a lot. He could be quite violent. I know that photo shows me swinging the spade, but it didn't make contact. He just stumbled and fell," said Lucy, repeating the words Jo had told her to use.

"I see," replied the chief constable as his eyes returned to the photo. He tapped the bottom right-hand corner. "The time shown here is ten minutes past ten. At ten thirty, your housekeeper, erm Jane?"

"Joan, sir," supplied Jo swiftly.

"Joan stated that she spoke to you in the kitchen of Hartwell Hall."

"Yes, she'd come to fill my freezer, bless her. We didn't know if we'd be able to see each other during lockdown and she knows I'm a terrible cook," Lucy began to explain then quickly shut up as Jo shot her a warning glance.

"And your friend, the local schoolteacher, was also there with you." This time Lucy simply nodded. "Then I agree at least in part with you, Spencer. Even if Rupert Hanley did die in the grounds of the Hayloft. I don't see how his wife could been involved in moving his body to the cave that night."

"She was still the last person to see Hanley alive, sir," argued Spencer.

"Actually. Sergeant, I would suggest that title could belong to our photographer here. Guy Lovell. A man who has recently been found guilty of several crimes concerning Lady Hanley and whose obsessive behaviour clearly stretched back to the time of Lord Hanley's disappearance. These photos place him at the scene, and he had the motive and quite probably the strength to not only kill but also to move Hanley by himself."

Lucy held her breath. This is exactly the point Jo had wanted to make. To give Spencer another name to go after, but her boss was doing the job for her.

"Did he have an alibi for that evening?" the chief constable asked.

"He told us he was at home discussing defence committee business with Seb Devizes, his special adviser, sir," replied Dawson promptly.

"So, Seb Devizes supplied his alibi as well as these photos. If anyone should be here for questioning, I'd say it's him. Sergeant Spencer, I told Inspector Palmer I had misgivings about you coming here when the Hanley investigation was closed. You have failed to prove the two men connected to the stolen guns were ever in North Yorkshire, let alone in Hartwell. Today's events feel like you are clutching at straws, and I shall be saying as much to your superiors in the Met. Ormond, can you arrange the release of Mr Harrison? According to the call handlers, half of Hartwell have phoned to say they saw him in the pub on the night in question. The last thing we need is them all turning up to make a statement."

Lucy had to really struggle to stop herself whooping with joy.

"I'll see to it straight away, sir," said Jo, then nodding to Lucy and Caroline: "Why don't you follow me down to the custody suite," she continued sounding very formal.

As soon as the three of them were out of earshot, Lucy let

out a huge sigh of relief.

"Oh my goodness, Jo that was amazing. It worked out just like you said it would. How did you know Devizes had given his photos to Spencer?"

"A hunch," replied Jo with a flicker of a smile. "We had a lucky break with the chief turning up like that, and that he remembered so much about the original investigation. Spencer couldn't argue with him."

"Dawson was great too."

"He was. I think I may have underestimated him."

"As appalling a man as Guy may be, I can't allow him to take the blame for something I did." It was the first time Caroline had spoken since arriving at the station and Lucy had never heard her voice sound so weak and shaky.

Jo didn't look at her as she replied. "I don't think it will come to that. The CPS won't think there's enough evidence to charge him. Even if they did, he'll never stand trial. Devizes might get charged with providing a false alibi, which would serve him right—the smug, arrogant sod."

By now they had arrived in the custody suite, Lucy and Caroline hung back and waited in silence while Jo went to speak to the sergeant on duty. She returned to them after a few minutes.

"He should be here soon. They're just completing the paperwork."

"Oh, Jo, that's wonderful! I'll never be able to thank you enough."

Jo opened her mouth as if she was about to reply, but instead the colour drained from her face, and she crumpled to the floor in a heap. Caroline immediately dropped to her knees and attempted to bring Jo round, gently shaking her, and saying her name over and over again, as Lucy screamed for someone to call an ambulance.

The ambulance arrived at the exact moment Rob was released. Lucy had rushed over and flung her arms around him.

"I can't believe you were going to take the blame. You could have been sent to prison," she whispered in his ear, aware they were still surrounded by police hurrying towards Jo.

"You're worth it," he whispered back. "What happened?" he asked, suddenly noticing Jo.

"I don't know. One minute she was talking to us, then she collapsed. I've been trying to call Jack, but he isn't picking up."

They watched as Jo was carried out on a stretcher. Lucy was torn between wanting to stay with Rob and be with her friend.

"Go with her," Rob insisted. "I'll keep trying Jack and come and find you."

CAROLINE AND LUCY sat side by side on plastic chairs in the hospital corridor. A fluorescent light flickered above their heads. Dawson had driven her and Caroline to the hospital, following the ambulance carrying the semi-conscious Jo. Jack had arrived ten minutes later, looking terrified. They had watched silently as doctors and nurses hurried in and out of the room she was being treated in.

"I wish you had told me. Not only about what happened with Rupert but about everything," Lucy said finally.

"I thought I'd dragged enough people into my problems."

"You sound like Jo. She's very good at keeping people at arm's length or at least she was before she arrived in Hartwell. You know, the more I think about it, the more I realise how alike the two of you are."

"We are certainly both fond of you, even if I haven't always shown it. I'm very pleased you decided to withdraw from the election. I would have missed you and Freddie very much if you had moved to London."

Lucy smiled. This was by far the nicest thing Caroline had ever said to her.

"I only stood in the election to get funding for the Rosemary Centre. What I don't get is why Devizes passed those photos to Spencer, when his family's bank had already set up the funding. Do you think it was because I said I was backing Heather?"

"The endowment came from me, or rather from Joseph's estate. He named me and his aunt as executors in his will. We set a charitable trust up in his name and donated to those causes we thought he would approve of. The Devizes Merchant Bank arranged the anonymous donation. It wasn't for entirely altruistic reasons though. I didn't want you to leave Hartwell."

Lucy was struck dumb for a second. She really didn't think there was anything else that could shock her today, then she remembered something more that had been said.

"What else haven't you told me? What did Shirley mean

about you being ill?"

"I have cancer. There's no cure."

Her mother-in-law's voice was calm, and she stared straight ahead.

"I'm so sorry, Caroline," said Lucy quietly. "I should have realised something was wrong. I did wonder why Meera seemed to be visiting you so often."

"Dr Kumar has been trying to persuade me to undergo treatment for my condition."

"I wish you would at least try."

"I don't deserve to live any longer. I killed one of my children and rejected another, and I wasn't brave enough to publicly admit either until today."

"I think you are the bravest person I know. You only did what you did to protect us all," protested Lucy. "Jo from Alexander, and me and Freddie from Rupert. I feel sick thinking about what could have happened to us if you had let him get his hands on that gun. We both know what he was capable of. If you won't have treatment for yourself, will you at least consider doing it for Freddie? He loves you very much."

Caroline gave her head a brisk nod and she blinked rapidly as her eyes filled with tears. Lucy reached across and took her mother-in-law's hand. Her skin felt thin and papery.

"I know we haven't always seen eye to eye, but you've been an excellent granny. Don't you think it would be wonderful if you could meet your new granddaughter?"

Down the corridor a door opened, and Jack suddenly appeared. The two women sprung to her feet and hurried towards him.

"How is she?" she asked.

"Okay. A bit weak. Her blood pressure is still low. That's why she fainted."

"And the baby?"

"They are still running some tests, but the heartbeat sounds good, and the scan didn't show any problems."

"Oh thank goodness," gasped Lucy throwing her arms around him.

"I want to go and phone Mum and let her know. I thought I should go outside to do it in case my mobile interferes with any of the equipment Jo's hooked up to. Will one of you go and sit with her?" he asked.

Lucy turned to Caroline. "Why don't you go?"

"She won't want to see me. She didn't want to speak to me in the car—she could barely look at me. Not that I blame her at all."

"You won't know if you don't try," prompted Lucy.

"It's times like this you need your mum," added Jack.

Caroline's eye filled with tears again. "She told you?"

"She did."

Caroline took a deep breath, slowly opened Jo's door and stepped inside.

CHAPTER EIGHTEEN

J O LAY WITH her eyes closed, listening to the beep of the monitor she was wired up to. Her left arm was sore where they had taken blood for various tests and her forehead was bruised from where it had hit the floor as she fainted. None of that mattered though. All that mattered was that her baby was okay. In the ambulance, she'd convinced herself there must be something very wrong. She could barely bring herself to look at the screen when they took her for a scan, and it had taken several minutes for the radiologist and doctor to assure her all was well.

Then the doctor had started talking to her about the possible causes of her low blood pressure and the tests they wanted to conduct, but she hadn't really listened. All she had wanted to concentrate on was the squirming image on the screen and the strong, steady heartbeat of her little girl.

At the click of the door handle, she opened her eyes expecting to see Jack, but instead it was Caroline standing there. She stepped into the room and took a seat in the blue plastic chair next to Jo's bed. Jo turned her head away. She hadn't let herself think about everything she'd been told as she sat by the fire in Lucy's library. After all these years, to have the story of how she'd come into this world revealed in a matter of minutes had been too much. Her brain hadn't been able to take it in, and instead she'd focused on what she knew best—her work and getting Rob out of trouble.

For what felt like a very long time, neither of them said a word. Finally, Caroline broke the silence.

"I knew as soon as I saw you." Her voice was so quiet, Jo was forced to turn and look at her so she could hear what she was saying. "It was your eyes. As soon as I saw those green eyes I knew. You have your father's eyes." Then she had felt Caroline softly place her hand over her own. Jo could feel the cool, smooth skin touch her own warm flesh, bruised from the drip that had been put in her vein. The realisation suddenly hit her. This was the first time she'd ever felt her mother's touch. Hot tears fell from her eyes on to the white, paper pillow. Silently, Caroline took a tissue from the box on the stand by the bed, reached over and gently wiped her face.

"What was he like?" Jo asked between sobs.

"Wonderful," replied Caroline simply. "And he was so happy when I told him I was expecting you. He wanted us all to live together at the Grange. He thought Alexander would understand." Her voice cracked. "I'm so sorry for leaving you. I really did think it was for the best. Alexander had already taken Joseph from me. I couldn't risk him harming you too. If I tried to leave him and keep you with me, I was sure he'd find me. Joan even offered to look after you, raise you as her own, but I was scared the truth would come out one day. Removing any connection between us seemed like the best way to protect you."

Caroline, who Jo had only ever known to be controlled and measured, sounded frightened and so unsure, just like she must have been all those years ago. Jo took a deep breath and managed to gulp back her last sobs.

"I understand," she said.

Caroline stared at her for a moment. Her pale blue eyes filled with tears too and her lips trembled. "I wish I could believe that, but I don't deserve your understanding or your forgiveness."

Jo opened her mouth. She wanted to explain that she knew that fierce feeling of needing to do everything in your power to protect the life growing inside you, that she could only imagine how desperate Caroline must have been, but before she could find the right words, Jack opened the door and Lucy followed him in, carrying paper cups of tea for them all.

"Oh my goodness, Jo! You gave us such a fright," declared Lucy swooping down to plant a kiss on Jo's forehead.

"Sorry," muttered Jo. As she handed out the cups, Lucy's gaze darted anxiously between Jo's tear-stained face and the damp tissue Caroline was holding.

"But everything is okay, isn't it? Jack told me everything is fine with you and baby Charlotte."

Jo looked from her friend's slightly strained smile, to Jack's concerned face, to Caroline's hand still holding her own. Suddenly she knew exactly how to convince her mother that there was nothing to forgive.

"Charlotte Caroline," she said quietly. "That's going to be her name. Charlotte Caroline."

Caroline's hand flew to her mouth and Lucy immediately burst into noisy sobs. When Rob arrived a few minutes later to collect Lucy and Caroline, he found all four of them in floods of tears.

CHAPTER NINETEEN

I T WAS DARK when Rachel finally returned to the cottage. After Jo, Caroline and Lucy had dashed off to the police station, she had stayed back at Hartwell Hall, to help Joan keep Freddie distracted. In between watching the latest *Jurassic Park* film, she had discreetly telephoned Dan, her uncle Frank and anyone else she could think of who might be able to support Rob's alibi. Then the call came from Rob himself to say that he had been released, but Jo had collapsed and was now in hospital. She and Joan waited until Lucy finally let them know that she and the baby were all right and Jo was being discharged.

As she stepped through her front door, she felt exhausted from all the worry, but also from the nagging little voice in the back of her head that wouldn't shut up. She flicked on the light switch and jumped when she saw Sarah sitting on the sofa. Her knees were drawn up beneath her chin and she had a blanket over her shoulders.

"Why didn't you call me?" she asked. Her voice was quiet and her eyes red-rimmed.

"Did you give Spencer that spade because you wanted to get Lucy and Rob into trouble?"

There. The nagging little voice had spoken. Sarah stared

at her for a moment then slowly nodded her head. Rachel felt sick.

"Why?" she asked. "Why would you do that? They've both been so kind to you. Especially Rob—he couldn't have been more understanding. He never once pushed you to finish the dig, so he could sell the Hayloft."

"I know, I know. It wasn't really about him. It was about Lucy. When Spencer started asking questions the other day, I wondered if he thought Rob and Lucy could have been involved in Rupert's death. If they had been an item secretly while he was still around. I found the spade and..." she paused "...I thought I'd found a way to get her out of our lives. It feels like she's always in the background. Like she could pull you away from me at any time."

Rachel felt anger rise inside her. "That's so stupid. And it wasn't Rob or Lucy who threw it down there it was me. If he'd continued not to defend himself, I would have to have told the police that—and it could have been me in the cells."

Sarah stared at her. "You threw it in? Why? When?"

"The night Rupert disappeared. Lucy met him outside the Hayloft and told him she didn't want him to stay with her at the Hall during lockdown. He turned violent and she used the spade to defend herself, then ran. When she returned to the Hall, she was terrified she'd killed him, so I went to check. There was no sign of Rupert, but the spade was still there, and it had blood on it, so I threw it where I thought nobody would find it."

"You see," Sarah's voice cracked. "She does have a hold over you. You incriminated yourself for her and you never told me."

"I was trying to protect you. If what I'd done ever got out, I didn't want the police asking you questions and you feeling you had to lie for me. But I was honest, when I told you how I used to feel about Lucy and that it was all in the past. She does not have a hold over me. I don't regret what I did for her, and I would do it again if I had to—and not only for Lucy. I would do the same for you or for Meera or Jo if they needed me to. You are all an important part of my life here in Hartwell."

"I know that," said Sarah quietly.

"Do you? Because you don't seem to want to get involved with any of them. It's like you say you want to be part of Hartwell, but you're not interested in the people here, and it's the people that make the place, every bit as much as the history and the old buildings and the legends. I love you and I really thought we had a future here, creating the heritage centre, building a life together."

Sarah threw off her blanket and leapt to her feet. "That's what I want too. I've let my jealously of Lucy get in the way. I know it sounds childish, but I wanted you all to myself. I've never been any good at sharing." There was a note of desperation in her voice as she reached out to Rachel. "I'm so sorry. Please give me another chance."

"It isn't me you owe an apology to," snapped Rachel shrugging off Sarah's hand on her arm. "Rob and Lucy are both back at home by the way, in case you were wondering."

Sarah stepped back as if she'd been slapped. "I was going to ask. I'm sorry. I guess I was so focused on you and me."

"Maybe that's the problem." Rachel sighed. The anger that had been simmering away had suddenly subsided.

"What are you saying?"

Rachel shook her head. Her temples were throbbing. "I don't know. I'm tired. I don't want to talk any more tonight, but if you are serious about us having a future together, you need to find a way to make things right. I have to know that you understand how important my friends are to me and I'd really like them to be important to you too."

She turned and headed towards the stairs, before stopping and looking back.

"By the way, we found out Joseph's mystery woman was Caroline. Jo is their daughter."

With that she trudged upstairs, tugged off her clothes and collapsed into bed. She listened for a moment, but it didn't sound like Sarah was going to follow her. Rachel didn't know who she was angrier with, Sarah or herself. Meera wasn't the only one who was guilty of avoiding a confrontation. She had chosen not to deal with the simmering resentment Sarah felt towards Lucy. She closed her eyes with one of her mother's many pieces of advice ringing in her ears: "Never go to sleep on an argument."

WHEN SHE WOKE up the next morning, there was no sign of Sarah. Quickly, she checked the wardrobe and gave a sigh of relief: her clothes were still hanging there. Downstairs she found a note. *Gone to York. Back soon. Love you.* Rachel's first reaction was relief, then she felt a stab of irritation. Couldn't she give work a miss for once? Not wanting to wait for Sarah to return, she went over to the farmhouse. After all the drama of the previous day, she hadn't spoken to her mother properly. However, instead of Mary, she found Becky folding a pile of laundry.

"You're optimistic if you think you'll be wearing a bikini in Hartwell anytime soon," she commented wryly.

"Soon I won't be in Hartwell," replied Becky without looking up.

"Why? Where are you going?"

"Goa."

"Goa?"

"Yes. It's in India."

"I know, but why are you going?"

"Nish has got a job out there. He's going to be running a bar on the beach and I'm going to help him. We're leaving straight after his sister's wedding."

"You won't be here for Christmas?"

"No."

"What about Minty?"

"She's coming with me of course. Nish's contract is for two months at first, but if things work out, it could become permanent."

"Are you serious?"

"Yes, why shouldn't I be? What do you want me to do? Stay here, where people will always wonder if I knew what Max was up to? Always that sense of suspicion, even from my own sister."

Rachel opened her mouth to protest, but Becky was in full rant.

"I can't live like that, and I don't want Minty to either. It's time for a fresh start for both of us."

Rachel stared at her for a moment. The expression on Becky's face was daring her to argue back, but instead she took a breath. Up until a few months ago, this was exactly what she'd wanted too, to leave Hartwell and travel somewhere exotic and escape her problems. How could she blame her sister for wanting to do the same?

"That sounds great. We'll miss you, but I really hope everything works out for you."

Becky looked momentarily stunned before mumbling, "Thanks," then scooped the laundry into her arms and marched out of the room.

A few seconds later, Mary appeared. "Did you know about Becky going to India with Nish?"

"Yes, she told me a while ago. She wants a fresh start, and I can't say I blame her. It's going to be a real wrench saying goodbye to her and Minty, but it's only for a few months, and I can always go and visit them, especially now all this business is over. I can relax more, and of course I won't be running the farm."

"I can't believe you kept it to yourself. This and everything else."

"We all thought it was for the best."

"For who? You knew Jo was desperate to find her mother."

"Knowing wouldn't have made any difference to her health. Besides it wasn't my secret to tell. We each tried to convince Caroline to say something when we realised who Jo was, but she refused. I think she was frightened of being rejected, so we stayed quiet out of loyalty to her."

"There's loyalty and there's helping dispose of a dead

body. You could have got into serious trouble, Mum."

Mary gave her a knowing look. "As could you, but that didn't stop you trying to hide what could have been a murder weapon. I hope you haven't been too harsh on Sarah because she handed it over to the police."

Rachel shifted uncomfortably under her mother's gaze. Although she hadn't admitted so last night she knew she bore at least some of the responsibility for what Sarah had done. She'd known she had a problem with Lucy and had chosen to ignore it rather than have it out with her.

"She wanted to get Lucy into trouble. She thought she and Rob might have killed Rupert," she replied, knowing she sounded like a petulant teenager.

"An easy conclusion to jump to and I think it's obvious she's always been jealous of Lucy, and I have to say you haven't always helped the situation." Rachel opened her mouth to protest, but Mary silenced her. "You know Sarah loves you very much, but underneath that confidence and all those qualifications, I think she is quite insecure. I don't suppose it helps that you have been keeping secrets from her. Not that I'm one to talk."

"Did Dad know what you did?"

"About Jo? No?" admitted Mary. "Caroline hid herself away at the Hall when her bump began to show—we couldn't risk Alexander finding out. He was such a dreadful man." Mary shuddered.

"Why didn't Caroline leave him?"

"I think she was scared. She'd seen what Alexander was capable of and how he managed to get away with what he did. Besides, when she lost Joseph all the fight went out of her. I wish you could have known her before all this, when she first arrived here. She was so open and full of life. She really threw herself into village life, then Alexander began to show his true colours. Annabel had tried to warn her—she knew what he was like—but by the time Caroline found out herself, Rupert had arrived. She got a slight reprieve when he was posted abroad, then along came Joseph. He was handsome, kind, clever, but in a quiet way, not showy. He fell in love with her and the village. He even bought the Grange so they could stay in Hartwell and keep Rupert close to his family.

"Caroline absolutely blossomed when she was with him. After he died, she was never the same again—cold, distant even with us, but determined. She wanted to protect Rupert until she realised he needed protecting from himself more than anyone else. Then when Freddie came along her focus shifted to him." She gave her head a little shake as if lost in her memories. "Going back to your dad. When the time came for Caroline to have the baby, Joan and I said we were going down to London for a few days to stay with Annabel. We made some excuse about there being a concert or a show we wanted to see. If your father or Bill did suspect anything they never mentioned it."

"What about Rupert?"

Mary shook her head again. "It was late when Caroline called me. I snuck out after he'd fallen asleep and when I got back, he was still snoring." She smiled. "You know what a heavy sleeper he was. Joan wasn't so lucky with Bill. He wanted to know where she was going. She made up some excuse, but she hated lying to him. It's been a burden we have all carried. Shirley was convinced Reverend Davenport had seen her leaving the pub, but he never said anything."

A thought suddenly occurred to Rachel. "Is that why you decided to finish farming and are okay about Becky leaving? Did you think the rev might say something, now he's getting more confused?"

"Not necessarily him, although he has started talking about Joseph a lot recently. You see he was the last person to talk to him. He was adamant that he couldn't have taken his own life because he'd been so happy when they'd spoken. It really bothered him. Of course Alexander used his influence to get the verdict he wanted, but no it wasn't only the rev we were worried about. None of us are getting any younger. It was only a few months ago that I was getting tested for dementia. I couldn't shake the feeling that sooner or later, we would be found out, I even wondered if the guilt would be too much for Caroline as she became weaker. Despite the three of us pleading and Meera's best efforts she's still resisting any treatment. But to answer your question, yes, I thought slowly handing control of this place to you and encouraging Becky to make a new start would be best, in case anything did happen."

"I wish you'd told me all this before."

"I think we both need to be more honest with each other and everyone else."

Rachel nodded, then another thought occurred to her. "Meera doesn't know what happened yesterday. I should let her know. She'll want to check on Jo." Jumping up, she gave Mary a quick kiss, then headed back to the cottage.

THE MOMENT SHE put the phone down, she heard the sound of a car outside. A few minutes, later Sarah appeared in the kitchen holding a small cardboard box. Rachel didn't know if she was still feeling emotional from speaking to a shocked Meera, but she felt tears well up in her eyes.

"I wasn't sure you were coming back," she said, thinking how beautiful Sarah looked even with unwashed hair and dark shadows below her eyes.

"I left you a note to say I was going to York."

"An emergency at work?" she asked, unable to keep the edge out of her voice.

"No, I called into the university, but it wasn't really work. I thought about everything you said last night, and you were right. What I did was purely malicious. I didn't sleep thinking how much trouble I could have got you all into."

"Maybe I should have told you what happened that night," conceded Rachel. "I certainly should have talked to you about Lucy. I knew you didn't like me seeing her."

"Maybe, but it doesn't change the fact I have been jealous of all your friends, and I haven't made enough of an effort to join in with the village, so I wanted to make amends. First, I collected up all the letters between Joseph and the woman we now know is Caroline and put them in the right order. Then rather than keep them, I dropped them off at Jo's cottage. I thought it could be a way for her to learn about her dad, and perhaps she and Caroline could bond over them."

"Don't you need them for your research?" asked Rachel. Sarah hardly let anything come between her and her work, but she simply shrugged.

"I photocopied the important bits, but most of it is personal stuff. It should be with the woman he loved and his daughter."

Rachel nodded silently. Sarah was obviously trying her hardest.

"Then, this morning," she continued, "I went to see one of my colleagues. He's an English professor and he collects early editions of the Brontë sisters. I persuaded him to sell me a rare volume of Charlotte's poetry. I thought Meera would love it, and I know you've been struggling to find her a wedding present."

Rachel picked up the delicate leather-bound book. She couldn't have picked anything better. Sarah really did know her old university friend.

"She will absolutely love it. It must have cost a fortune."

"It doesn't matter," said Sarah, who was now blushing furiously.

"Thank you. It's perfect."

"I'm also going to ask Meera to recommend a counsellor. Someone I can talk to about my insecurities and trust issues."

Rachel reached over and gently placed her hand on Sarah's shoulder. "Really? That would be even more perfect than the book."

Sarah gave her a shy smile. "I'm not done yet. I've saved the best for last. My gift for Lucy. Will you come up to Hartwell Hall with me so I can give it to her?"

Rachel took her hand. "I'd love to."

SARAH CLEARED HER throat. Rachel knew she was feeling awkward and embarrassed, but Rob and Lucy were simply sitting with their arms around each other on the sofa, looking more loved up than ever and waiting expectantly to find out what this surprise visit was all about. Rachel was perched on the edge of the opposite sofa. She had no idea what Sarah was going to say.

"Recently," began Sarah, "my team and I have been spending time studying the Hartwell nobles. Particularly the inscriptions. We want to create a central exhibition around them, you see—after all who doesn't love a good legend?" She gave a weak smile and Lucy and Rob nodded politely. "We began translating the runic symbols in conjunction with the letters from Joseph Baxter Tarrant that Meera found in her attic. He believed the original translation, by a Victorian academic, was incorrect."

She then produced a photo of one of the Hartwell nobles that had been enlarged.

"The symbol that has always been thought to mean 'cursed' is actually upside down when the noble is held with the hart upright, do you see?"

Lucy peered at the picture Sarah was holding up and squinted. "Not really. They just look like a bunch of squiggles to me."

"It's that symbol right there—you see it's inverted." Sarah beamed at Lucy's blank face. "Inverted means the opposite. The same symbols are engraved around the edge of the well. Once we saw that, well, we knew for sure. Joseph's hunch had been correct."

Rachel could see she wasn't getting through to Lucy. "It means the Hanleys are blessed not cursed, Luce."

Lucy's perplexed face finally broke into a smile. "Really? Freddie isn't cursed? We had it wrong all this time? That's wonderful! Thank you so much, Sarah! Honestly, you have no idea what a relief this is."

Lucy sprang up and threw her arms around the blushing archaeologist. Then Rob stood up and shook her hand.

"Cheers, Sarah, this means a lot."

"That's all right," she mumbled. "I wanted to put Lucy's mind at rest. I know it has been bothering her."

"Will you both stay for a glass of champagne? After the last twenty-four hours we've all had, I feel ready to celebrate."

Rachel remained silent and raised her eyebrows at Sarah, who smiled and nodded.

"Yes, Lucy. Thank you. We would love to."

Rob rose to his feet. "You get the glasses, Luce. I'll get the fizz."

When Rachel and Sarah were left alone. Rachel went over to Sarah, wrapped her arms around her and softly placed a kiss on her lips.

"You were right—that was the perfect gift. From now on, I think you should be in charge of present buying for the two of us."

"That sounds good to me," replied Sarah with a smile. "I really am very sorry for the way I behaved."

"I'm sorry too. I should have been more supportive, knowing how you felt about Lucy."

Rachel kissed her again and pulled her down on to the large squishy sofa, then turned to look at her. Sarah's expression was inscrutable.

Rachel lowered her voice. "Is what you told Lucy true? Because we both know she and Rob, or probably anyone else in the village, are never going to read any academic papers you write."

Sarah didn't quite meet her gaze. "I know," she replied as out in the hallway came the sound of a champagne cork popping.

Chapter Twenty

MEERA HAD MISSED Joan's birthday party. Half an hour before she was due to leave Agnes had turned up unexpectedly and four days early. She had declared that the train companies charged more the closer they got to Christmas, and she wouldn't pay their inflated prices. Following her plan to give her future mother-in-law a second chance and see the best in people, Meera phoned Lucy to apologise then prepared something for them to eat. Remembering Agnes preferred simple food she made vegetable soup and served it with French bread. However, Agnes still complained that it tasted too spicy and the bread too crunchy. Then she took herself off to bed at seven o'clock, leaving Meera wishing she was with her friends instead.

The next day her own parents arrived to stay for the wedding too. Her mother wanted to give herself plenty of time to prepare the food and her father needed no excuse to spend time with his daughter and grandson. It was the first time both parents had met. Meera had made lunch for the four of them. Ben was out on call, covering for his colleagues, so he could take time off after the wedding, and Krish was in bed with a cold.

Things were not going well. Her mother, wearing a tight

smile, kept trying to start new topics of conversation only to be met with monosyllabic answers from Agnes. Her father had given up speaking all together and kept his head down, eating quickly, clearly wanting the meal to be over with as soon as possible. Meera was avoiding making eye contact with her mother, knowing she was cross with her for not confronting Agnes.

As they finished their main course in silence, the telephone out in the hall rang, and it was with some relief that Meera excused herself and went to answer it. It was Rachel. Meera knew straightaway something was wrong. Her normally unflappable friend sounded stressed and almost tearful as her words came tumbling down the line.

Almost ten minutes later, Meera put down the receiver and took a deep breath as she tried to process everything Rachel had told her. Rob being arrested, then released, Caroline admitting to being Jo's mother. Then Jo fainting again. She felt quite dizzy trying to make sense of it all. Instinctively, she placed her hand over her stomach. She hadn't allowed herself to get excited yet. Unlike Jo, she had a very regular cycle that she monitored religiously. She was late only by a few days and like Lucy had said she'd been under a lot of stress recently. It could be a false alarm.

"Meera! Are you serving dessert?" Agnes's shrill voice came through from the dining room. Meera didn't respond. What if it wasn't a false alarm? She thought about the colonel, who would have loved to have a family, but instead had chosen those he felt closest to, to bestow his beloved wife's jewellery on. Then she thought about what Rachel had just told her about Caroline, who had made impossible choices to protect those she loved. Finally, she thought about Jo, who must have been so scared to be so close to creating the family she'd never had only to almost see it snatched away from her. There was seeing the best in people and there was being a fool. She walked briskly back into the dining room.

"Mum, please will you keep an eye on Krish for me? Jo fainted and was taken to hospital. They have discharged her and she's back home, but I want to go and check on her."

"Oh my goodness! I hope she is okay," gasped her mother. "You go. Krish will be fine with us."

"Send her our love," added her father, who loved children and had been overjoyed when he'd heard Jo was expecting a baby.

"I thought you were going to tell me about this wedding of yours," huffed Agnes from the other end of the table.

"I don't think there is anything to say. Ben and I are getting married on Saturday. We want to be surrounded by people who love us and wish us well. If you don't feel you fit that description then perhaps it might be better for everyone if you didn't attend."

Agnes stared at her opened-mouthed, but Meera didn't wait for a reply. She grabbed her coat and car keys from the kitchen and hurried out the door. As soon as she stepped outside, she saw Ben driving towards her. She couldn't avoid speaking to him any longer.

He stepped out of his car with an easy smile. "Hello there, where are you off to in such a hurry?"

"Jo's fainted again. I want to check she's okay."

"Crikey! I hope she is. I thought for a minute lunch had

gone so badly you were running away," he joked then seeing Meera wasn't smiling, asked, "How did it go?"

"Not well." She took a deep breath. "I overhead your mother tell Belinda that she didn't think we should have children because and I quote, 'It would be far too confusing for the wee thing and it wouldn't know what it was'."

Ben's face dropped. He looked completely aghast.

"Meera! I'm so sorry," he stammered. "I knew her views were old-fashioned, but…" He paused and shook his head. "Did she say this today?"

"No, when she was here before. I should have told you, but well, I think I was hoping I'd been mistaken. I've just told her if she isn't happy for us she shouldn't come to the wedding. I'm sorry if you think I should have consulted you first, but I was upset after Rachel phoned to tell me about Jo."

"No of course not. I agree with you completely. Look, give me two minutes and let me see if I can sort this out."

He took her hand and led her back into the dining room where her parents and Agnes were still sitting in an icy silence. Her mother looked like she was bursting to say something, but Agnes was the first to speak.

"I've been told I'm not welcome at your wedding, Benedict. Is that the case?"

"That depends, Mother," replied Ben evenly. "Meera is under the impression you don't approve of our relationship, and that you don't believe we should have children. Is that the case?"

Meera saw her parents exchange a quick glance, then in unison, silently and diplomatically, they left the room. Agnes sat up very straight and placed her hands firmly on the table in front of her.

"It is. I don't approve of your choice of wife. In my opinion, she is the wrong race, wrong religion and she has already failed at marriage once. I can't say this wedding is anything to celebrate."

Meera was surprised she didn't feel more shocked or upset. Instead, she felt quite calm. At least she now knew that there was nothing she could have ever said or done to make the cold-hearted woman sitting at her dining table like her. Her own parents could be accused of being traditional or old-fashioned. They sometimes need to be cajoled into a more modern way of thinking, but they had experienced the pain of prejudice enough themselves to never subject anyone else to it.

She felt Ben let go of her hand and glanced across at him. She had never seen him angry before. He was always level-headed, reasonable, pragmatic, to the point where it irritated her sometimes. Even now there was no shouting or clenched fists, but his jaw had tensed, and his normally twinkling eyes had become cold with quiet fury. He turned to her and spoke quietly and calmly.

"Meera, you go and see Jo. I know how worried you are about her. I'll take care of things here. Drive carefully."

As she drove towards Jo's cottage, she wondered if she should also have told Ben there was a chance she might be pregnant. She knew he would be thrilled. But no, she didn't want to get his hopes up and today certainly didn't feel like the right time. She would wait a few more days, then take a test. If she got the result she was longing for she would tell him on their wedding day. It could be her present to him, but until then this was one last secret she would keep to herself.

Meera followed an exhausted-looking Jack up the stairs and into the bedroom. Jo was sat up in bed, with her hair hanging loose around her face. She looked younger and more vulnerable than usual. There was a purple bruise on her forehead and a small plaster on her hand. She smiled when she saw Meera.

"A visitor for you, Jo," announced Jack.

"Hello," said Meera giving her a gentle hug.

"I was going to take Baxter for a quick walk. Will you be okay? I'll only be a few minutes," Jack said.

Jo gave him an indulgent smile. "I've got my best friend who also happens to be a doctor with me. I think I'll be fine and don't rush back. Take the poor dog for a decent walk. He's barely been out—he must have his legs crossed."

"Yes, boss," he replied with a grin, then blew her a kiss before closing the door behind him.

"How are you feeling?" asked Meera as she settled into one of the kitchen chairs Jack had placed next to the bed.

"Okay I guess, all things considered."

"You've had quite a time of it, I hear. Rachel called and told me everything," Meera explained.

"My head is still spinning with it all, but the main thing is the baby is okay."

"And you can stop stressing about who your parents are,"

ventured Meera.

Jo smiled. "Yes, although it still hasn't really sunk in." She gestured to a pile of letters on the bedside table. "Sarah came over earlier and dropped off loads of stuff she had about my dad. Those are letters between him and my mum. I've asked her to come over and read them with me. Would you like to see a picture of him?" she asked shyly.

She handed Meera a slightly creased photo of a man, who looked to be about thirty. He had light brown hair, an open, smiling face and Jo's green eyes.

"I can see the resemblance. What a handsome man," she commented.

"He was clever too. Sarah said he was one of the leading archaeologists of his generation."

"And if he were still alive, I think he would be very proud of you."

"Really?"

"Of course. Look at the life you have made for yourself all on your own. You're a detective, for goodness' sake."

"A police officer is meant to uphold the law. I encouraged Lucy to lie to Spencer and the chief constable."

"You did what you thought was best," Meera assured her. She was worried now. This wasn't like Jo. She never doubted herself.

"You wouldn't have done it. You always do the right thing."

Meera took a moment before she replied. "Sometimes doing the right thing isn't as simple as it sounds. I thought about this when I gave conflicting advice to Krish. I've always told him to respect his elders, to be polite, but what if his elders have bigoted views? Should he remain silent or speak up? What you did hasn't caused any harm to anyone, has it? If Caroline and Lucy had told the truth who would have benefitted? Certainly not Freddie, an innocent little boy who might have been deprived of his mother and grand-mother. It wouldn't have brought Rupert back. We both know Lucy has suffered already, and I dare say the same is true of Caroline."

"Maybe you're right." Jo sighed. At that moment, there was a gentle tap on the door and Caroline herself appeared. It had only been a few days since Meera had last seen her, but she thought her face looked a little older but softer.

"I let myself in. I hope that's all right." Her smile faded when she saw Meera. "There isn't anything wrong is there?" she asked anxiously.

"No. I was only making a social call. I heard what happened and wanted to check she was okay," explained Meera as Caroline sat down in the chair on the other side of the bed.

"I'm fine," added Jo. "There's no need to worry. I've just been telling Meera about the letters."

"It was very kind of you to invite me," replied Caroline. She picked up the piece of paper on top of the pile and, turning pale, gasped. "Oh good Lord, this is the letter I wrote to him when he returned to London. He was only gone for a week, but I missed him dreadfully."

"It wouldn't have felt right reading them without you," said Jo softly, placing her hand on Caroline's arm. Meera watched the two of them in silent fascination. Both women were normally so detached, confident and self-assured, yet around each other they seemed nervous and vulnerable. They reminded her of Krish when he was trying to get close to a wild animal. They were cautiously tiptoeing along like they were scared of frightening the other one off. Caroline put the letter down and reached into her handbag. She produced a bundle of about thirty envelopes, neatly tied together with a pink ribbon.

"Actually, if you don't mind, I have some correspondence of my own I wanted to share first. I had asked my solicitor to keep them with my will, but I thought it would be better to give them to you now."

She gave Meera a quick glance and Meera wondered if the two of them had discussed Caroline's condition.

"What are they?" asked Jo as she undid the ribbon. Meera could now see each envelope simply read 'Jo'.

"Birthday cards," replied Caroline. "It may sound silly, but every year I bought and wrote you a card. I wanted you to have them after I had gone. I wanted you to know that I never forgot you. I thought about you all the time."

Jo's eyes filled with tears and Meera's own throat tightened. All of a sudden, she felt like she was intruding.

"I think I'll go now and leave the two of you to read together," she said standing up quickly. Jo brushed a tear away with the back of her hand.

"Sorry, Meera, I don't know what's wrong with me. I've cried more in these last twenty-four hours than I have in my whole life."

Meera bent down and hugged her again. "Don't apologise and don't be silly. It sounds like the two of you have a lifetime of tears to catch up on and hopefully some laughter too. Take care of yourself and I'll call in and see you tomorrow."

"I'll see you out, Dr Kumar," offered Caroline rising to her feet and turning to Jo who had begun carefully opening each card. "And I'll make us both a nice, strong cup of tea before we start on those letters. I have a feeling it's going to be rather emotional."

Meera followed Caroline to the front door, but before she stepped outside, Caroline placed her hand on Meera's arm.

"May I have a word, Dr Kumar?" she asked in hushed tones.

"Of course," replied Meera wishing for the hundredth time that she would use her first name.

"I hope you don't mind. I wouldn't normally bother when you are not at work, but I've been thinking about what you said, about the possibility of undergoing treatment. I think I'd like to look at my options, see if something might work for me."

Meera felt a surge of happiness. "That's wonderful news," she whispered. "I'm so pleased. Why don't you come and see me at the surgery on Monday morning, and we can go through everything then. Or if you prefer, I could arrange a referral and you could visit Mr Charnsworth again instead."

"No," replied Caroline glancing back towards the staircase, "thank you, but I don't want to go to London. I want to stay here in Yorkshire."

"Of course. I understand," replied Meera diplomatically.

Meera got into her car and watched in her rear-view mirror as Caroline closed the cottage door. After all these weeks she'd almost given up on Caroline ever accepting treatment. She smiled to herself. Perhaps miracles really did happen.

When she returned to the Grange, she found Ben in the kitchen, loading the dishwasher.

"How's Jo?" he asked.

"She's okay. A bit bruised and emotional."

"And how are you?"

"A bit bruised and emotional too."

"I'm terribly sorry, Meera. She's always been difficult, but I never imagined she would be so rude and unpleasant to you of all people. I wish you'd told me."

"Where is she?"

"On her way back to Inverness. I gave her a choice. Either apologise to you and change her attitude or leave. She chose the latter, so I called her a taxi."

Meera sat down with a sigh. She felt relieved, but disappointed. "I kept thinking I might be able to win her round."

Ben shook his head. "I don't think such a thing is actually possible. She drives everyone away. My dad stuck it out until my sister and I were grown-up, but he left her at the same time I went to university. And why do you think my sister lives on the other side of the world? It was partly to get away from her. She won't change. She's stubborn, but in the end, she's the one who'll lose out."

"But you won't have your mother at your wedding. Are you really okay with that?"

"I know this might sound terrible, but I'm actually relieved. Even before what she said today, I would have been worried she would offend someone. We've never been close.

Not like you and your mum, or you and Krish."

"How is he by the way?"

"Watching TV and eating ice cream with your parents. He seems to have made a remarkable recovery since my mother left," he said with a grin.

Meera smiled back at him. "Maybe I'm not the only one who feels like a dark cloud has lifted."

"True. Although that could be a bad thing considering you're hoping it will snow for the wedding."

Meera groaned. "Oh, Ben, I love you, but I really hope the jokes in your speech are better than that!"

Chapter Twenty-One

J O WALKED SLOWLY and steadily behind Meera. By some miracle the dress fitted her, but she didn't want to risk any sudden movements. She took her seat in the front row of chairs in the ballroom. The bride was stunning and the groom looked as though he might burst with pride. Lucy and Rachel sat on either side of her and behind her were Jack, Shirley and Caroline.

She'd felt three pairs of anxious eyes on her as she made her way down the aisle. This was the first time she'd ventured out of the cottage since she'd been discharged from hospital. Meera had been visiting daily and monitoring her blood pressure to make sure it didn't drop too low. She had also warned Jo what felt like a hundred times against taking hot baths or standing up too quickly. Meera hadn't been Jo's only visitor and the little cottage was crammed full of flowers from friends and colleagues. Dawson had arrived and shyly presented her with a huge box of her favourite chocolates and even the chief constable had paid her a visit.

"Looking forward to having you back when you're feeling up to it, Ormond," he'd said cheerfully. "I'm planning on setting up a rural task force. I'd like you to head it up, if you're staying that is." He produced an envelope from his inside pocket. "This arrived for you from Inspector Wallace. I imagine she wants you back on her team. Can't say I blame her—you are an excellent officer."

Jo took it and murmured her thanks. This was what she'd been waiting for since she'd arrived in Hartwell, the chance to return to London, but now it was in her hand she didn't feel the expected surge of excitement. Before arriving in Hartwell, her work had been her life, but now everything had changed. She had good friends here, and Jack, she had found her mother and was going to become a mother herself. She had created a new life in more ways than one. Did she really want to give it all up? What for? The chance to work with people like Spencer again? The chief constable had looked around the room as he stood up to leave.

"You've got a nice place here. It brings back quite a few memories. I lived in the cottage next door when I was the village bobbie, back in the days when such a thing existed. Strangely enough I was involved in investigating the death of another young man back then. In fact, I discovered the body down by the old well. It was a gunshot wound. The verdict was suicide, but I had my doubts—not that anyone would listen to a young, inexperienced constable. I always wondered what really happened, but I suppose I shall never know the truth, a bit like the Hanley case. It seems Hartwell is a place destined to keep its secrets."

After he'd gone, Jo slipped the envelope into the drawer of her bedside table without opening it. For the first time in years, she'd barely thought about work. When she'd opened her eyes and found herself in hospital, all she could think about was her baby. The relief she'd felt when the doctors had told her all was well was something she'd never experienced before.

Not wanting to start crying again she pulled her thoughts back to the wedding. Meera and Ben gazed at each other as they exchanged their vows while Krish, who was acting as Ben's best man, looked on shyly. Jo glanced around the ballroom. The place looked amazing after the film company's Jane Austen makeover. It was lit entirely by candles that flickered and reflected in the mirror-covered walls. It wasn't a large gathering, only about fifty people or so. Ben and Meera's colleagues from work had all dressed in Regency outfits, while Meera's family were all wearing dazzling jewel colours. Even the colonel, in his bright red dress uniform and minus his crutches, had made it.

"It looks like the early days of the Raj!" she'd heard Lucy gasp under her breath as they walked in. There had been a slightly awkward moment when Reverend Davenport had arrived. He had strode to the front of the room and addressed everyone with 'dearly beloved, we are gathered here today,' until Belinda had swiftly ushered him to his seat. The only person missing was Agnes. It seemed that Ben had been unable to get the horrible woman to apologise. Not that it seemed to be bothering him too much.

Jo watched as with a broad smile he slipped a simple gold band on to Meera's finger. She and all the other guests burst into spontaneous applause. The ecstatic bride and groom made their way back down the aisle and out into the grand reception hall with its black and white marble floor, where the official photographer was waiting for them.

Jo, Rachel and Lucy followed them out and waited to be

called for the group photos. Away from the candles, Jo had a chance to properly look at Lucy. For once, her friend didn't look her usual stunning self. Although still beautiful, her eyes were a little bleary and her skin less glowing than normal.

"You're not pregnant too, are you?" hissed Jo.

"No," Lucy hissed back. "Hungover."

"Did you and Meera have a hen night without us?" joked Rachel. Jo and Lucy laughed. Meera, the world's greatest worrier, had strictly enforced a total ban on any sort of hen or stag celebrations. 'I don't want any mishaps' had become her mantra.

"No," said Lucy. "Rob and I went to the count last night and watched Heather win the election. I may have enjoyed a few too many glasses of fizz in celebration. I was pleased for her of course, but it was wonderful to see that smug grin wiped off Devizes's face after what he tried to do to us."

Rachel's hand flew to her mouth. "Oh my God, what with everything else that's been happening, I completely forgot about the election."

"And you, a member of our parish council," teased Lucy.

Suddenly, there was a squeal of excitement. Meera who was now posing on the impressive cantilever staircase, had thrown her bouquet into the air and Sarah had caught it. A blushing Rachel raced over and flung her arms around her.

"Anyone want to take a bet on the next wedding we'll be attending?" asked Jo.

"Oh, I hope so," sighed Lucy. "I really like Sarah. Did you know she worked out what all those marks on the Hartwell nobles mean? Apparently, the Hanleys aren't cursed, we're blessed."

"That's great news," agreed Jack, who had come to join them, but Jo shook her head.

"It's good news for you, but maybe not for the heritage centre. A curse is better box office. If I was Rach and Sarah, I'd keep quiet."

Jack reached over and tapped the end of her nose affectionately. "There's my cynical Jo!" He turned to Lucy. "She's been getting quite sentimental recently, crying at soppy adverts on the TV. I've been worried about her."

Jo grinned at him. "Maybe I'll be a bit of both from now on, cynical and sentimental."

After the photographs, there was a buffet served in the dining room. It had been made by Joan and Meera's mum. A combination of Yorkshire and Punjabi foods, sausage rolls and pakoras, cucumber sandwiches and onion bhajis that sounded weird, but somehow worked.

Following the meal, there was dancing. The string quartet that had been playing classical music while they all ate had now switched to pop tunes. It had sounded crazy when Meera had described it to her, but like the food, it was perfect. After Ben and Meera's first dance, the others took to the floor. Rob spun Lucy expertly around, Nish and Becky only had eyes for each other, Sarah and Rachel shimmied in unison, even Caroline and the colonel managed a surprisingly impressive waltz.

Not feeling up to dancing herself, Jo stood and watched as Meera's father—with tears of happiness streaming down his face—took his daughter in his arms and began proudly twirling her around the dance floor. She turned to Jack who was by her side and whispered, "Can we sneak out for a few minutes? There's something I need to do."

Thick feathery snowflakes were beginning to fall again as she made her way up the path through the churchyard. Meera would be pleased, she thought. She'd been praying it would snow for the photographs.

"Be careful. The path could be icy," Jack shouted out from where he was waiting by the car. He'd wanted to come with her, but this was something she needed to do alone. Halfway along the path she stopped next to the grave of Annabel Marsden, the colonel's wife. Jo removed a single white rose from her bouquet and rested it against the headstone of the woman whose house she had been born in.

The gravestone next to the wooden bench looked like it had been dusted with icing sugar. Pulling down the sleeve of her jacket over her hand, she knelt down and carefully brushed the snow off the inscription. She'd never really paid much attention to it before although she'd sat in this spot countless times. Slowly, she ran her fingers over his names and dates until they were numb. He was only a little older than her when he'd died. No. He was only a little older than her when he was murdered.

"Hello, Dad," she said softly, as she laid her bridesmaid bouquet on his grave. For the first time since hearing Caroline's story, she allowed herself to imagine what her life might have been like had her father lived. Growing up with two parents who loved and wanted her. She wouldn't even have minded having Rupert as a dysfunctional half-brother. It would have been better than being alone.

She slipped her hand in her jacket pocket and brought out the letter the chief constable had given her. She crumpled it up and laid it next to the flowers. Then retrieving a lighter she still had in her jacket, she set it alight and watched it burn. The flames melted the snow and the smoke smudged the white petals. Within a few seconds all that was left was a small pile of ashes. To Jo this tribute to the father she would never know felt every bit as appropriate as the roses and gardenias. Her past was behind her. She was finally home.

THE END

The Secrets of Hartwell series

Book 1: *Four Hidden Treasures*

Book 2: *Four Secrets Kept*

Book 3: *Four Silences Broken*

Available now at your favorite online retailer!

More Books by H L Marsay

The Lady in Blue Mysteries
Book 1: *The Body in Seven Dials*

The Chief Inspector Shadow series
Book 1: *A Long Shadow*

Book 2: *A Viking's Shadow*

Book 3: *A Ghostly Shadow*

Book 4: *A Roman Shadow*

Book 5: *A Forgotten Shadow*

Book 6: *A Christmas Shadow*

Available now at your favorite online retailer!

About the Author

H L Marsay always loved detective stories and promised herself that one day, she would write one too. She is lucky enough to live in York, a city full of history and mystery. When not writing, the five men in her life keep her busy – two sons, two dogs and one husband.

Thank you for reading

Four Silences Broken

If you enjoyed this book, you can find more from all our great authors at TulePublishing.com, or from your favorite online retailer.

TULE
PUBLISHING

Printed in Great Britain
by Amazon